Jordan

The
Executioner's
Daughter

The Executioner's Daughter

LAURA E. WILLIAMS

Henry Holt and Company ❧ New York

I want to thank Christy Ottaviano, amazing editor, wonderful person.

I'd also like to thank the Ryskiewicz family. Without their friendship,
the research would have been close to impossible.

And thanks to Sherrilyn Kenyon for knowing so much.

Henry Holt and Company, LLC
Publishers since 1866
175 Fifth Avenue
New York, New York 10010
www.henryholtchildrensbooks.com

Henry Holt® is a registered trademark of Henry Holt and Company, LLC.
Copyright © 2000 by Laura E. Williams. All rights reserved.
Published in Canada by H. B. Fenn and Company Ltd.

Library of Congress Cataloging-in-Publication Data
Williams, Laura E. The executioner's daughter / Laura E. Williams.
p.   cm
Summary: Thirteen-year-old Lily, daughter of the town's executioner
living in fifteenth-century Europe, decides whether to fight
against her destiny or to rise above her fate.
[1. Fathers and daughters—Fiction.   2. Executions and executioners—Fiction.
3. Middle Ages—Fiction.   4. Fate and fatalism—Fiction.]   I. Title.
PZ7.W666584 Ex 2000   [Fic]—dc21   99-049259

ISBN-13: 978-0-8050-8186-2 / ISBN-10: 0-8050-8186-0 (paperback)
ISBN-13: 978-0-8050-6234-2 / ISBN-10: 0-8050-6234-3

First published in hardcover in 2000 by Henry Holt and Company
First paperback edition, 2007

Printed in the United States of America on acid-free paper. ∞

1   3   5   7   9   10   8   6   4   2

This one's for Rick Kiernan, my husband.
He knows why.

The
Executioner's
Daughter

CHAPTER ONE

Lily loved early morning best of all. The time before the sun rose and melted away the mist. The time before even her parents stirred in the far side of the cottage. The time when only she was awake and free to wander without anyone making a fuss.

In the warmer months, she roamed the edges of the forest for plants to renew her father's supply of medicines. This morning she gathered yarrow, agrimony, horsetail, and wild lettuce, carefully laying the sprigs and leaves in a wide, flat basket she carried over her arm. Walking along, she found herself looking at the sky as much as at the ground. Her mother said that was why she was clumsy and fell so often.

Above her, the trees rustled in the late summer breeze. She shaded her eyes against the glare of the sun, watching the slender shape of a dove circle above her before winging out of sight. She loved doves, as did her mother. Their mournful call and their gentle ways. Lily smiled, imagining herself flying free.

When the high walls that hid most of the town came into view, she stopped. Only the church spire and Lord Dunsworth's castle on the far side could be seen above the turreted barricades. Lily didn't care for the town or the dirty moat. Nor for the narrow roads that twisted and turned like a pit full of serpents. She stayed away as much as possible, preferring the solitude of the forest, though she had to be wary of the cutthroats and thieves that hid in its murky depths and assaulted travelers. But even the fields where the farmers now threshed grain, or the meadows where animals grazed and shepherds kept watch were too crowded for her.

"There it goes!" someone shouted in the distance.

Lily whirled around, her outer tunic catching a puff of air and billowing around her legs. Those boys again! Town boys. And they were headed across the meadow in her direction. In another moment they would see her. Fear left her mouth dry. Lily took a giant step toward the bushes, nearly tripping over her skirts, looking for a place to hide. Without time for thought, she flung herself into a thicket of brambles. She winced as she landed on a sharp stone. Thorns scratched her face, but at least she was hidden. And just in time, too.

A rabbit raced by, the boys not far behind. The animal dodged left then right and suddenly disappeared. The boys nearly fell over each other, stopping so suddenly. They stood in a gasping huddle right next to her hiding place. Lily barely dared to breathe.

"It got away," one of the boys said, still trying to catch his breath.

"It can't have gone far," the smallest one said. "I jabbed it good, right in the leg."

A third boy laughed. "I'm sure you missed it, John. You're always thinking you've killed the rabbit or cornered the pheasant, but you never catch a thing."

All the boys laughed now. The littlest one stomped his foot. "You'll see, sodheads. I'll get that rabbit and have it for supper, too!"

"Enough," one of the older boys said. "This isn't fun anymore. Leave it and let's find something else to do."

"But I stuck it good and now someone else'll get the rabbit," the one named John protested.

The boys looked about. Lily didn't move, not even to brush aside a spider crawling up her arm.

"Come away," the first boy said, throwing down his stick. The others did the same, all except John. "There's no one here to find your skinny rabbit."

The smallest boy blinked back tears and glanced around, staring a moment too long into the thicket. Lily felt like he was looking straight at her, but then he turned away.

"Let's go find Maggie and Eunice," the tallest boy said.

"But I thought you wanted to play with me. What do you want girls for?" John asked, twisting his stick between his small hands.

"They make good targets," Tom said with a grin. "Come with us if you like. If you can keep up." The boys laughed and trotted off toward the gates of town.

After one last look into the thicket, John gave up on his rabbit and ran after his friends.

Lily waited till they were out of sight before she moved. Better they should pick on Maggie and Eunice than a poor rabbit, she thought as she pushed her way out of the brambles and undergrowth. She brushed dirt from her palms and plucked some thorns and twigs from her tunic. Before she retrieved her basket of herbs, she picked up the deserted sticks the boys had sharpened roughly on stones, cracked them in half over her knee, and tossed them aside. With her basket over her arm, she bent down and looked closely at the grass, peering this way and that until she found what she was looking for.

With her first finger, she dabbed at the blood on one of the leaves. The little boy had stuck the rabbit after all. Slowly, carefully, she followed the scattered red trail to a mound of brush not ten lengths away. Quivering behind a barricade of dead branches, a small brown rabbit twitched its nose at Lily as she got down on her knees and reached forward. She grabbed the animal by the scruff. The rabbit kicked feebly, and then went still.

Lily cradled the injured animal. "I'll make you well," she crooned. "Don't worry about those evil boys. I won't let them harm you again."

"That's my rabbit," a sharp voice called behind her.

Lily turned. John the youngest stood there, feet wide, pointed stick gripped in both hands. He jabbed it toward Lily as if she were an animal to be tamed.

Lily dodged out of the way. Fear tightened her throat, and her voice sounded squeaky. "I thought you went with the others."

"I tricked you," the boy said. He kept his gaze

lowered to the tips of her shoes. "Now give it over. 'Tis mine."

Lily shook her head. "You left it here to die and I found it. 'Tis mine now." She glanced around nervously, wondering if the other boys were far behind but she didn't see them. One small boy couldn't hurt her, not the way a crowd of them could, like the last time they'd cornered her.

The boy's tousled brown hair stuck out at odd angles, and his leggings were held up by a rope tied around his waist. And though he scowled at her feet, his dirt-streaked face puckering above his brows like an old man's; Lily saw the tremble of his lower lip.

She clutched the rabbit closer and lowered her voice to a raspy growl. "Do you know who I am?"

The boy's eyes flickered up at her, but he tried to set his quivering lips firmly. "You're Lily White as Bones," he finally managed. "Gallows Girl. You're the executioner's daughter, but"—he took a deep breath—"but I'm not afraid of you."

"Foolish boy!" Lily stared at him hard, till she thought her eyes might have crossed, giving her a truly evil glare. He took a step backward, holding the stick in front of him. "You should be afraid of me," she went on. "If I ever catch you again . . ." She let her voice trail off menacingly, waiting for the waif to run away, crying.

But he only took another step backward and said, "I want my rabbit. I've got to show Tom and the others. Show them I really did stick the rabbit like I said. They'll never believe me else."

"I'll not give it over!" Lily rasped louder.

John's eyes filled with tears.

Forgetting to give him the evil eye, Lily snorted with disgust. "Do boys always cry so much?" she demanded in her usual voice. She tried to ignore the pinch of pity she felt for him as he blinked back his tears. He was a town boy, same as the others, cruel and heedless. How many times had children just like him brought tears to her own eyes? But no more. Her tears had only meant harsher taunts, so she had learned not to cry. Never to cry.

The boy hastily wiped the back of his hand across his eyes. "I'm not crying. 'Tis dust, is all. Now give me my rabbit."

"Nay, you'll not have it," Lily said. With that, she turned and ran as fast as she could, cradling the rabbit in her arms.

She took a shortcut through the forest, dodging trees

and leaping over fallen branches. Her basket bounced on her arm, scattering its contents as she raced on. Lily glanced over her shoulder twice. The first time to see the boy trailing behind her. The second not to see him at all. She turned abruptly north, away from the direction of the town gates, and followed a path she'd made from her frequent walks in the forest. At last she slowed her steps, catching her breath and taking a look at the rabbit in her arms. It lay limp, blood staining its hind legs, but Lily felt the delicate thrumming of its heart beneath her hands. There was hope yet.

At last she reached the small cottage she shared with her father and mother outside the town walls. Her father had built their home in the midst of some willow and ancient evergreens, which kept it sheltered and out of sight from all but the most curious. The wattle and daub walls were sturdy, and the thatch roof overhung the sides all around to better shed the rain. Beyond their patch of land spread out fields of wheat to the front and side, and forests to the rear. Not far away on the right rose the tall, thick stone wall that circled the town like protective arms.

Their cottage contained one room with a trestle table near the hearth, a few benches and stools, cooking utensils, a bed to one side, and a curtained-off corner for Lily. Attached to the cottage, her father had built a small chamber, which he called his apothecary. Here he kept his herbs and remedies and special tools. Often she found her father and mother there, side by side, working without speaking.

Lily scattered the chickens and ducks out of the way as she neared the cottage door. Her dog barked a greeting, straining on the rope that kept her in the yard.

"Hush up, Blossom," Lily said. "I'll let you go in a bit, I promise." She entered through the back door, directly into the apothecary. "Look what I've found."

Her father turned away from his table and frowned at the rabbit. "What poor hunter maimed this animal and didn't kill it properly?"

"And the herbs you were to collect?"

Lily looked at the empty basket over her arm.

Her father knew her well enough and didn't wait for a reply. "The usual boys from town," Lily said. "They chased it with sticks and stones."

"What happened to your face?" he asked.

Lily bowed her head over the rabbit. " 'Twas nothing," she said. "I tripped and fell into some prickers."

Lily's mother, Allyce, brushed willow bark powder from her fingers. She had hair the color of sunlight, and skin so white it seemed to glow. Without a word, she took Lily's chin to lift her face to the light, then she angled it this way and that. The skin around Allyce's lips tightened. "You must be more careful," she said gently.

"Aye," Lily agreed.

Her father turned back to his work. Allyce held her hands out for the rabbit. "Let me see." With soothing movements, she inspected the frightened animal. Lily watched, wishing her own touch was as soft and comforting, but she had hands like her father; strong and wide, and oftentimes clumsy.

"Can we save it?" Lily asked after a moment of silence, broken only by the scraping of her father's pestle grinding against the mortar.

"Hmmm," Allyce murmured. "I suppose we have half a chance to save the wee thing, which is better than no chance at all."

Lily nodded. "I'll make a poultice."

Her mother pointed to a couple of herbs, then she placed the rabbit in a basket loosely woven out of twigs and meadow grass.

Using the herbs her mother had suggested, Lily mixed self-heal and chickweed in a wooden bowl before adding water to form a warm mash.

Allyce inspected the medicine and nodded approval. "Get your friend."

Lily carefully retrieved the rabbit from the basket. *Her friend.* It was true that her only friends were the animals she brought home to care for. But at least they couldn't call her names, and if they ran from her, it wasn't because she was the executioner's daughter.

"Hold it still, child," her mother reproved, applying the poultice to the wound.

"I'm trying," Lily said, wishing again she had her mother's calming way. Animals wild with pain, children screaming, or crying men and women alike were soothed by Allyce's touch.

"Very well," her mother murmured.

Lily smiled, humming softly to the rabbit. Slowly it relaxed in her hands as her mother applied more poultice and then wrapped the injured leg with a scrap of cloth.

"It should heal properly," Allyce said, wiping her hands on her apron.

Lily squeezed the rabbit with happiness. Suddenly it struggled to get free. She fumbled, trying not to drop the animal on the floor. "Oh," she cried, "I've loosened the bandage."

Allyce tightened it again and patted her daughter's shoulder.

Lily sighed. "I'll never be like you. You could

pick thorns from a unicorn's muzzle and it wouldn't run away."

"Have patience, child. You have a gentle heart, and the rest will come. Now go put the wee one outside with the others."

Lily took the rabbit outside where she had stacked cages for her injured friends. She fed and petted her collection of rabbits, one quail, a pheasant with a broken leg, and a fox who'd been half torn apart by dogs when Lily had found him over a fortnight ago. Now he scampered around in his cage and licked her fingers when she poked them through the wooden bars.

"You'll be leaving me soon," she said to the young fox. "Only, stay away from those vicious dogs, do you hear?"

When she was done, the sun hung low, casting long, violet shadows to the east.

Inside, her father sat on a bench by the unshuttered window, polishing his ax with a soft cloth. William Goodman was a large man with broad shoulders and wavy black hair. His sharpening stone sat at his booted feet. Laid out on the bench beside him was a knife with a narrow blade, a sharp hook, and a tankard of ale. Lily knew it wasn't her father's first drink. Nor would it be his last.

Allyce stood by the cook fire, stirring their supper in a large iron kettle. Her thin back curved over the pot like a willow branch, and her cheeks glowed red from the heat.

Lily took the long-handled spoon from her mother. "Let me," she said. "I like to stir."

"Thank you, child," her mother said, wiping the sweat from her brow with the hem of her apron. She moved to the trestle table and laid out wooden bowls, chunks of hearty wheat bread, creamy butter, and cheese curds.

"More ale, gentle Allyce," Will said, holding up his tankard, using his favorite name for his wife.

"You've had enough," Allyce said firmly.

In a burst of temper, Will slammed the tankard beside him on the bench. "I'll have more and plenty," he bellowed.

Allyce didn't flinch. "You won't be fit for the evening chores."

"I'm fit enough," Will said, his voice back to its low rumble.

Lily watched as her mother reluctantly filled the

vessel and her father near downed the refill in two long draughts. Allyce pressed her lips together and turned away, placing the jug of ale on the table, out of Will's reach. But Lily knew that wouldn't stop her father from finishing the jug and likely refilling it a time or two more from the keg before he fell into bed and snored the night through.

Silence fell over the cottage. Her father drank every night, so Lily was used to it. But occasionally he drank far more than usual, and she didn't like how it made him angry and raise his voice. And yet other times it brought tears to his eyes as he sat in the corner, near weeping into his tankard.

"The ale is a balm to his soul," Allyce had once told Lily.

"Like a poultice for a wound?" Lily had asked.

"Aye," agreed her mother.

"But what's wrong with his soul?"

Allyce had sighed and pulled Lily close in her arms. "One day you'll see and understand. But not for many years I hope."

Lily had wanted to ask more questions, but her mother shushed her.

Remembering, Lily swung the pot off the fire and

ladled the soup into the bowls. She wondered if souls could bleed like flesh, and if so, what had cut her father so deeply that he needed ale every night to soothe the ache.

"Come to the board," Allyce said to Will when Lily was done filling the bowls.

"First, I must finish my task," Will said. "I'll not have my blade dull tomorrow."

Lily looked at her mother, noticing how distraught and frail she suddenly appeared.

Allyce looked at her daughter and nodded. "There's to be an execution tomorrow." She lowered her gaze. " 'Tis the fourth one in as many months. Seems Lord Dunsworth is finding great use for the executioner this year."

Lily silently agreed. In the past, there had been only two or three executions a year. "What did the condemned man do?" she asked.

"Poaching," her father said. "Killed and butchered a doe from Lord Dunsworth's woods. Foolish man. I don't know how he thought he wouldn't get caught with soldiers prowling about as they do." Will swallowed the last drops of ale from his tankard and moved to refill it.

Slowly, Lily ate her supper. Her mother wouldn't allow her to watch tomorrow's execution, she knew, even though the whole town would be there for the spectacle. She could barely remember the last execution she had attended, the only one, when she had been a mere seven years. Four thieves were sentenced to hang together. Out of town, on a hill, the townspeople had built a gallows large enough to hang all four.

Everyone had gone to the hanging. Lily had been told to stay behind, but she longed to be a part of the laughing, shouting crowds she heard on their way to the execution. She had joined them, hiding amongst the milling people to keep hidden from her parents—just another child off to see the hanging.

But all she could remember when she got to the hill was looking up at the distant gallows, squinting against the sun, and hearing the roar of the crowd all around her. On the platform, a tall man, who wore a black hood and black gloves like her father's, looped nooses around the thieves' necks and pulled the ropes till the condemned men hung like sacks of grain.

CHAPTER TWO

The next morning, when Lily came back from her foraging, she found her mother kneading bread at the table, her sharp elbows pointed out to either side like broken wings. Allyce glanced up. Already she looked weary from the day. On execution days, or days they were summoned by Lord Dunsworth's bailiff to the dungeon, her mother always looked older and sadder.

"Good day, Mother," Lily said, trying to sound bright and cheerful, as though she could bring the fresh morning in with her. She lay aside her basket to help her mother with the dough. "Did you sleep well?"

"Well enough," Allyce said, brushing a strand of hair from her face with the back of her floury hand. "Take the mattress out today and give it a good beating. Something bit me harder than usual last night."

Lily nodded and picked up some dough and began to push it this way and that. The warm lump felt good in her hands. After a few moments of silence, she asked, as she always did, "Did you dream?"

Her mother dreamed every night. Usually she told Lily her dreams, which were fanciful and full of color and light. But sometimes she just crossed herself and wouldn't speak of her dreams, as though they frightened her to even think of them. And occasionally, after something happened, like her father accidentally cutting off the tip of his little finger with his ax, her mother said, "I saw it in a dream."

Allyce pounded the dough on the board, punching it with her fists before dropping it into a bowl and covering it with a towel. Then she moved on to the next lump.

"Well, did you?" Lily prodded her mother.

Allyce cast a sideways glance at her daughter. "Aye, I dreamed a dream," she said, "of you, if you must know."

"Me?" Lily smiled. "Was I a princess this time or a unicorn or a . . ." Lily closed her eyes, imagining what magical creature she could be. "Or a gentle dragon, mayhap?"

Her mother snorted. "Nothing so wonderful this time, daughter," she said almost sharply. "You were a fish."

Lily gasped, "A fish? With slippery scales and the stench of the fishmonger?"

This time her mother laughed. "I don't remember smelling you. But you were a fish with stripes of many colors. A fisherman caught you in his net. You were so beautiful, he didn't know what to do with you. Finally he let you go and you swam away, out to the great, wide sea . . ." Her voice trailed off.

Lily frowned. She preferred the dreams of herself as a princess courted by a prince of the realm. A unicorn was better than being a flip-flopping fish, even if it was a beautiful one.

"Is that all?" Lily asked, thinking her mother must have more to tell her. Perhaps she turned into a princess later in the dream.

" 'Tis all," Allyce said. "Now go see your father and then collect the eggs, and I'm sure Milly is ready to burst."

Disappointed that there was no more to the dream, or at least no more her mother would share with her, Lily wiped her hands clean, then took the basket of fresh herbs and pushed through the leather curtain into the apothecary where her father was preparing tincture of thyme.

He looked up at her before returning to his work. "Mistress Smith will come today to pick this up for her colicky babe," he said.

"I could have made it," Lily said. "I remember how."

" 'Tis no matter," Will said. "It keeps me busy until it's time."

To go to the execution, Lily finished silently for him.

She placed the basket on the long trestle table. She would sort and chop and dry the herbs later. Without another word, she went out the back door and collected speckled eggs, finding them hidden in dark hollows around the dirt yard. Next, she tied Milly to a stake with a bit of rope and milked the goat into a wooden bucket. For cow's milk, they depended on farmers giving it in trade for medicine and healing. Often the farmers traded milk or a newly slaughtered pig, cow, or chicken. Or sometimes a wheel of cheese or a sack of grain or, even better, flour. The townsfolk also gave goods, as well as coins if they were wealthy enough.

Lily untied Milly, and the goat kicked off across the yard, scattering squawking chickens. Laughing, Lily carried the milk inside and poured it into the churner, where she would later turn it into cheese.

Her mother and father sat at the table, breaking their fast. Will tore at chunks of day-old bread, dipping the hard crust into cider to soften it. Allyce nibbled on a piece of cheese.

"Sit," her mother said.

Lily scooped some hot porridge into a bowl and sat beside her mother, reaching across the table for some clotted cream.

"Mind your elbows, child," her mother said absently.

Lily held back a sigh, but did as she was told. Though why manners mattered when they never had guests, nor were invited anywhere to dine, made no sense to her. Still, her mother insisted on them. No elbows, no spitting, no talking with a full mouth. The hardest rule was not to feed her dog at the table. Blossom had to wait till after the meal for scraps, no matter how sweetly she begged.

They ate in silence, as they often did. Afterward, Lily scraped the wooden bowls into a slop bucket for Blossom. The dog snorted and slobbered as she licked it clean. Lily grinned. She had a strong suspicion that her dog was carrying a litter.

Her father picked up a large, leather bag. The

innards clanked dully, drawing Lily's attention away from happy thoughts of pups scampering about the yard. Lily stared at the bag, envisioning the contents. The hood, the ax, the various knives and hooks. Only once had Lily asked what they were for.

"The ax is for hands and—" her father had begun before Allyce cut him off with a sharp elbow in the arm. "She'll need to know these things," he'd said, frowning at the interruption.

"Not yet," Allyce had said, interrupting yet again. And though she was a small woman, she had prevailed, and no more was said about it.

Lily knew the tools were for executing and punishing the wicked and unholy. She knew her father, with her mother's help, vanquished evil. And though he was not allowed in church by the townsfolk, surely there would be a place for him beside God for ridding the land of criminals who sinned against the holy Lord above and the lord of the castle.

"Stay close to the cottage while we're gone," her mother warned Lily as she trailed out the door behind her husband. She looked as though she might say more, but then just pressed her lips together and left, leaving the door wide behind her.

Lily watched them move down the rutted path, her father tall and broad, clutching the bag over his shoulder with his black gloves on, and her mother barely taller than herself, her head bowed as though in prayer. Lily closed the door and made her way to the apothecary. For the rest of the morning, she tried not to imagine what was going on in town. Did the criminal cry for mercy? Did the crowds cheer as they did at the hanging years ago? There was no one to ask.

❧   ❧   ❧

Lily baked the risen dough, filling the cottage and even the yard with the nutty scent of fresh bread. For her midday meal, she ate warm slices of bread spread with fresh goat cheese, washing it down with a mug of cider.

Just as she finished tossing a crust to Blossom, a soft sound came from the back door. Lily jumped. If her parents caught her feeding the dog food that had not gone stale, there would be extra chores for a sennight at least.

The scratching sound came again. Lily hurried through the apothecary and opened the back door. Mistress Smith stood in the shadow of the door frame, her face partially covered with a veil. The woman slipped into the room quietly, glancing back over her shoulder to make sure no one had followed her.

Lily was used to people acting skittish. For as long as she could remember, folks had come to request help and healing from her father, and from her mother, too, but usually under the cloak of night or in secret during the day. Today most people would be at the execution and wouldn't notice Mistress Smith slipping away.

"I have the tincture," Lily said, moving to get the medicine her father had left for the woman. Normally, Lily was told to stay in the cottage when her parents attended to an injury or illness in the apothecary. But lately, she had been asked to do small things like make simple tonics or administer medicines when her parents weren't at home.

The blacksmith's wife gratefully took the small flask that Lily held out for her. "My babe is fretting," she said.

Lily noted the dark circles under the woman's eyes, proof of long nights awake with a colicky child. She nodded warmly. "This thyme will calm her. Come again if you need more," Lily offered with a smile.

The woman looked grateful and tucked the flask in a

pocket pinned to her overdress, then she handed Lily an arched piece of metal. " 'Tis a new handle for your pot. Your mum said she needed one and that it would do for payment."

Lily inspected the handle. " 'Tis well made," she said. "Thank you kindly."

Mistress Smith smiled shyly, then looked around nervously as though she would be caught chatting with the executioner's daughter. With a quick bob of her head, she slipped outside and hurried up the path and out of sight.

Lily shrugged. Her animals were her friends, but it was pleasant to talk to someone once in a while. Someone who could talk back with more than a squawk, bark, or purr.

As she stood in the doorway, she noticed a flicker of movement off to the side. Blossom noticed, too, and dashed over to the bush, barking insistently. Living outside the town walls, they had to be vigilant about thieves, but thieves tended to avoid the executioner even more than other folks, so Lily had little fear as she approached.

"John the hunter!" she said in surprise when she made out the shape hiding inside the branches.

"Get your dog away," the small boy cried, fear stretching his voice thread thin.

"Blossom!" Lily commanded. Blossom sat and wagged her rear with excitement.

The boy crawled out of the bush, not bothering to brush the dust from his knees or hands. He stared at the ground and shifted uneasily. Though he was quite small, Lily decided he must be around seven years.

Finally Lily said, "If you've come for your rabbit, you'll not get it."

"Where is it?" John craned his neck to look around Lily, but she moved purposefully to block his view.

"You may as well go home now." She raised the hand that still held the new handle. The boy flinched as though he expected her to hit him with it. Hastily she lowered it to her side.

"I want to see my rabbit," he said stubbornly.

" 'Tisn't yours."

" 'Tis so."

"Nay!"

The boy glowered up at her, apparently forgetting his fear in the midst of his anger. "Fine! 'Tis your rabbit! I just want to see what you've done with it."

"You promise not to come back and steal him in the middle of the night?" Lily asked.

The boy's eyes widened. "Sneak out of the gates in the dark?"

Lily snorted. Of course not! She'd forgotten that the townsfolk were all frightened of their nighttime shadows.

"Then come along," she said. "This way." She led John to the arrangement of cages she kept on the side of the cottage where they were hidden from view.

His mouth dropped open, amazement replacing his fear. "Are they all yours?"

"Nay. I'm just caring for them till they can run off on their own." She moved to the cage holding the rabbit and tenderly lifted it out while John looked on.

"You saved its life?"

Lily nodded. She didn't usually think of what she did as saving lives, but she liked the sound of it. "Aye, I am a healer like my parents, only I heal animals instead of people."

The frightened look returned to his eyes at the mention of her parents. "They're not home yet, are they? I saw them at the execution."

"Aye, 'tis where they are," she said abruptly. She put away the rabbit. "They'll be home very soon."

The boy didn't need another hint. He fled.

Lily brushed her hair over her shoulders. She didn't

want a boy nosing around here anyway. He would just be a nuisance and probably try to steal the animals when she wasn't watching. She tossed her head, glad to be rid of him, and walked around to the front of the cottage.

She was just about to enter when her mother trudged toward her down the path. "Did you see anyone along the way?" Lily asked, unsure of how her mother would feel about her visitor.

Wearily, Allyce shook her head. "Just a shadow here and there. Did Mistress Smith come by for the medicine?"

"Aye," Lily said, following Allyce inside. She wondered if her mother longed to have friends. She didn't even have a collection of animals to talk to, and Lily's father wasn't one to waste words on idle chatter.

Her mother passed her into the apothecary, going straight to the bucket of water they kept in the corner. Using the strong soap that burned Lily's nose, she knelt down and scrubbed her hands all the way up to her elbows as she always did after an execution. She used her fingernails to scrape at her skin.

"He deserved to die," Lily said. "He was a thief." Her voice rose as her mother continued to wash, scratching at her hands till they turned as red as the blood she was trying to wash off. "He was a vile sinner who had to die! Father said so."

"Judge not lest ye be judged," her mother snapped. And then in a softer voice: "Do not judge so harshly, child."

"But Father says—"

"Aye, Father says much," Allyce interrupted, "but he doesn't know all. No one does. Not I, not you, not even Lord Dunsworth."

Lily stood silent. She might not know all, but she did know when it was futile to argue with her mother.

At last, Allyce stood up from the bucket, holding her dripping hands before her. "Father will be home soon. Help me lay out supper."

Lily followed her mother through the apothecary and into the cottage. How was it possible to judge a criminal too harshly? she wondered.

CHAPTER THREE

Lily watched her mother as they prepared the evening meal. As her mother chopped and sliced, she seemed to lose the tension from her face and shoulders. She was even humming by the time they were through.

Once the table was set and supper was heating over the fire, Allyce took Lily's hand. "Come walk with me."

Lily smiled. She and her mother often used to walk together with Allyce pointing out herbs and flowers and telling Lily their medicinal uses. But lately, her mother hadn't had time. Or perhaps it was more a matter of desire.

They took the path Lily had made along the edge of the forest. "There is a cluster of yarrow," Lily pointed out.

"Aye," Allyce agreed. "And yonder some wolfsbane. That, you must—"

"Never pick because 'tis poisonous," Lily finished for her mother with a laugh. "I remember your lessons well," she assured her.

The two wound around trees and cut across corners of fields. Lily didn't fear a taunting crowd of children with her mother beside her.

Allyce suddenly stopped walking. Without a word, she looked up to the sky. Above them circled a pair of doves, their tail feathers pointing out behind them.

"How beautiful," Allyce said softly.

They watched silently as the doves flapped off toward the town.

Hand in hand, the two continued to walk aimlessly, heading deeper into the forest. The rotting leaves from seasons past cushioned their steps. When they came to a stream, Allyce lay back on the mossy ground. Lily sat by her and wove a garland out of twigs and ferns she found around her. When she placed it on her head, she felt like a princess wearing a crown.

"Have you ever seen a princess?" she asked her mother.

"Nay. Where would I have a chance to see a princess? Or a prince? I've not even seen the King. Only Lord Dunsworth. And he's not such a sight to see."

"But you've seen knights," Lily said.

"Aye," Allyce replied. "At the castle they come and go. They are rather common, in fact." She said it as if she were describing a type of rat.

Lily laughed. "Are they all brave and handsome?"

"Nay, they fart and spit like any other man."

Lily groaned and threw a fern at her mother, who batted it away. "Tell me true," she begged.

"I don't know what is true, daughter. I've only seen them from a great distance. They are not interested in the likes of us," she said flatly.

Lily gently tugged off her crown and tossed it into the stream. She watched it slide over rocks and tumble through rough water until it was whisked around the bend. She tried to imagine its journey, but she had never been farther in the forest than the old stones from the days of the Druids, nor had she ever crossed the meadows to see what lay beyond. But if she were a garland, sweeping down the stream, or even better, a bird flying high . . . She took a deep breath. What use was there in imagining such impossible things?

She lay down beside her mother and stared up at the evening sky that winked at her from between the over-head leaves. "How did you meet Father?" she asked, her voice sounding barely louder than a puff of air.

For a long moment, her mother said nothing. Lily thought her mother hadn't heard her, but she didn't want to ask again. Her whole life she'd known that her parents didn't like to talk about the past. She had come to accept this silence, but sometimes she longed for a history. Something more than the story of how the midwife wouldn't attend when Allyce's time was near, so Will had had to act as midwife and help bring Lily into the world. "The best midwife in the land," Allyce always said at the end of the story, making Lily laugh and her father wince.

"He saved me from my fate," Allyce said slowly, breaking into Lily's thoughts. "Your father was my own knight, though his armor was black as death."

"What do you mean?" The words were barely out of her mouth when her mother sat up in alarm. Then Lily heard the clop of hooves hitting an occasional rock and the clank of buckles and harnesses. Fear shot through her. All travelers in the forest had to be careful, but especially a woman and her daughter, alone and unprotected.

They sprang to their feet. Allyce grabbed Lily's hand and lifted her skirts with the other. They started running. Lily heard a shout behind them, and her mother pulled her along faster. Whenever Allyce glanced behind her, Lily caught a glimpse of her fearful eyes and two bright spots of color on her cheeks.

Lily opened her mouth to breathe easier, but still each breath came ragged. She swiped her hair out of her face, tripped over a log and sprawled forward. The air was knocked out of her.

"Come along," Allyce panted. "Quickly now."

Lily staggered to her feet. Once again her mother took her hand and they ran. The jangle of harnesses seemed to come from many directions, and the pounding hooves beat into her body until she didn't know if it were the horses or her own heart she heard thumping.

When they neared the clearing where they lived, they didn't slow until they'd burst out of the forest. Gasping for air, Allyce bent nearly double. Lily held her arm. She tried to listen for the sound of pursuit, but all she could hear was the deep in and out of her own breathing.

At last their racing hearts slowed and Lily wiped a sleeve across her forehead. Allyce placed her hands on Lily's shoulders. "We must not tell your father what happened, do you hear?" she said.

Lily nodded. She was used to keeping secrets. She

no longer told her parents when children chased her or if a farmer's wife had come upon her unexpectedly and spit at her. As for telling others, whom would she tell?

Allyce hugged her. "Father is home now. Let me go in first. You tend to your animals and come later."

Lily made her way to the side of the cottage. Now that the danger had passed, anger sparked in her. It seemed she was always running away from something. More like *someone*. Taunting children, farmers who chased her if she got too close to their fields, and men on horseback who could be soldiers of Lord Dunsworth's or thieves. Running away. It seemed that's all she knew how to do. That and picking herbs.

She examined the cages to be sure they still held strong. Then she changed the water and left seeds and wilted lettuce to hold the animals over till morning. Thinking enough time had passed, she went inside.

Her father sat in a dark corner. When Lily came in, her mother called them to the table to eat. As her father rose out of the shadows, Lily was shocked to see that he still wore his gloves. While her mother scrubbed her hands raw after an execution, her father simply removed his gloves and placed them on a high shelf.

Several years ago, Lily had teetered on a stool to bring them down and play with them while her parents were busy in the apothecary. But the gloves were stiff, and Lily had been afraid to do more than nudge them with the tips of her fingers.

Looking up from the table where she sat, Allyce stiffened when she saw her husband's hands. "Take them off," she said, her voice as sharp as a nettle.

Lily winced to hear the harsh sound, so unlike the sweet, happy voice her mother had used only a short time earlier when they had wandered through the forest.

Her father said nothing as he poured himself more ale and swallowed the entire tankard in one breath.

"Take them off," Allyce said again. "I'll not sit here while you wear them." She stood abruptly, nearly knocking over the bench behind her.

"Why should I?" Will demanded, sounding like his voice might burst through his chest at any moment. "I'll need them again tomorrow!"

"What? Nay . . ." Her mother sank back onto the bench. Her shoulders seemed to drown in her dress as understanding swept over her.

Lily reached a hand toward her, but her mother

flinched away. Hurt by the rebuff, Lily clasped her hands together under the table.

"Aye," Will said. "The bailiff sent word that there's to be another execution."

Lily picked at the food on her small trencher as she watched her father quickly drain and refill his ale a few times over. He didn't eat, and neither did her mother.

At last, Allyce pushed herself to her feet and passed beyond the leather curtain into the apothecary.

Her father stood unsteadily and went out through the front door. A few minutes later, she heard the loud thwacking sound of him splitting wood. Lily peered out the window and could just make out his figure in the darkness. Every time he raised the wood ax, he shrugged his left shoulder, as though that gave him more power. And he kept his head tilted to the side as he did whenever he was concentrating. The tankard of ale sat on a log next to him, within easy reach.

Lily moved away from the window and cleaned up the table. Blossom whined, and she shooed her outdoors, then she peeked around the curtain to find her mother.

In the gloomy light with only a couple of candles

flickering nearby, Allyce stood before the long table sorting piles of herbs. Lily watched for a minute before she realized her mother was simply moving one pile from place to place. Then her mother stopped and leaned against the table, holding herself up with her hands splayed against the wood. Her shoulders shook with silent sobs. Lily longed to rush to her mother and hold her, but what comfort could she give? She could barely calm a wounded rabbit, never mind ease her mother's grief.

Uncertain, she stood watching, waiting for a sign that her mother needed her . . . wanted her, or even knew she was there. But Allyce didn't turn around. Slowly her slender shoulders stopped shaking. They squared, and Allyce took a deep breath, and then another.

Lily's chest felt tight. "Mother?" she said at last.

Her mother turned toward Lily, her eyes wet. She opened her arms and Lily ran into them, wishing she could loosen the tears that strained at her throat. But she had worked too long and too hard at keeping them trapped inside and she didn't know any longer how to unstopper the opening to let them flow.

"Dear Lily," her mother crooned, rubbing her back.

ıst wanted to comfort you," Lily said against
ther's shoulder.

so you do." Lily heard the warm smile in her
voice. "You are my greatest comfort."

n why are you sad?"

ıl the things I must do in this life," Allyce said
avily. "The executions, the tortures, the—" She
paused abruptly and pulled Lily even tighter against
her. "I pray that you never have to—" Again she cut
herself off.

"Never have to what, Mother?" Lily asked.

Allyce shook her head. "Pay me no mind, daughter.
'Tis fate." She gave a short laugh that scratched at Lily's
ears. "Sometimes I think I cheated fate, and now fate is
laughing at me."

Lily understood that fate had a hand in all that happened, but she didn't understand how her mother
thought she had cheated it. One did not cheat fate or
change one's destiny.

"You have me," Lily said, her voice small, afraid this
would not be good enough.

Her mother squeezed her harder.

They stood for a long time in the circles of each
other's arms. Lily remembered back to when the only

place she found solace was cuddled up next
mother. Her father, so big and dark, often frigh
her, though he was never cruel to her. Sometime
was even kind, bringing her treats and tickling her
she curled into a giggling ball.

But until recently, her mother had always been like a
blanket, keeping her warm and safe. And that's how she
felt right now. Yet Lily also felt protective, as though
she too held the power to soothe and comfort.

⁂ ⁂ ⁂

The rain started early the next morning, so that when
Lily awoke, it was to its patter on the thatched roof of
the cottage. She lay on her pallet, listening. It was a
good and proper day for an execution, she thought.
Somehow it didn't seem fair to put someone to death
when the sun blazed merrily in the sky and the birds
sang sweetly. But on a dreary day, when the sky cried
for the wicked, it seemed right and just.

Then she remembered her father's drunken raging of
the night before. He'd chopped wood deep into the
night, taking rests only to quench his thirst. Well after
moonrise, he'd stumbled into the cottage, demanding
more ale. He had smashed his tankard on the table
so hard, the handle broke off. Then he'd thrown the

43

fire, scattering coals and sending sparks

the cottage.

the ale?" he had demanded.

drunk it all," Allyce had said stiffly.

dark, Will had swept the bowls and jugs off
ety shelves. He'd knocked away a stack of bas-
nd tipped over the empty washtub in his futile
ch for more to drink.

Lily had trembled behind her curtain where she hid. Her father had seemed cruel and desperate, not the quiet man who gave medicines and good advice to those who came for help. Not even the sullen man he'd become of late. This raging man, she did not recognize.

When at last he'd given up searching, his legs buckled beneath him as he sank onto a bench. Only the faint glow of the embers had illuminated his features. He'd rested his elbows on his knees and buried his face in his hands.

Allyce had gone to him and placed a hand on his shoulder. "Come, William," she'd said calmly.

Clumsily he'd risen, leaning heavily on his wife. She'd led him to their bed, where he lay down with his boots on.

"I am cursed," Lily had heard him say in a hoarse whisper. "And I've cursed you, too."

"Sleep," Allyce had said, and she'd started humming a melody that had nothing to do with curses or despair or drunken rages.

So when Lily awakened the next day with the rain in her ears, her mother's song still played in her heart.

CHAPTER FOUR

The sky wept all through Lily's morning chores. She closed the shutters against the chill, but soon it was too dark to see, so she opened them and wore a shawl to ward off the cold. She moved buckets throughout the cottage to catch the rain that dripped in through loose patches in the thatching.

During a lull in the rain, Lily went outside to collect the eggs and milk Milly. When she rounded the side of the cottage, a ghostly figure hunched by the cages.

"Oh!" she cried, nearly dropping the egg basket. Her sudden fear turned to anger. "Who said you could come here, sneaking through the fog like a thief?"

"I wasn't sneaking. I was just standing here."

Lily eyed him suspiciously. She noticed he had his

fingers in the fox's cage the way she often did. "Where are your friends?"

"Who?"

Lily moved the egg basket to her other hip. "The boys you hunt rabbits with."

"They're all at the hanging."

"Why aren't you?"

John shrugged.

Lily shifted her weight from one foot to the other. "Want to help me find the rest of the eggs?" she asked, surprising herself as much as the boy with this question.

After a moment of awkward silence, the boy replied, "Nay," in a scoffing voice.

"I'm not going to let you stand there while I work. Do you want to clean the cages?"

John's face slowly lit up. "Aye."

"Do you think you can do a fine job?" Lily asked doubtfully.

"I can!"

Turning to hide her smile, Lily showed him what to do and went about with her egg collecting and milking. When she was done with Milly, she helped John finish up.

"The fox is soft," John said, poking his fingers back into the kit's cage.

"I think he likes you," Lily said, enjoying the way the boy's face beamed with pleasure.

John laughed. "I think so, too."

The rain started to fall again. "I have churning to do, so go on home," Lily said.

"May I come again?" John asked. "I mean to help clean."

Lily tilted her head and considered for a moment. "You may come," she finally agreed.

He flashed his crooked teeth at her and then scooted off into the foggy rain.

Lily watched him go before making her way into the cottage. She wouldn't dare call him a friend. He was merely a pesky boy. But he said he'd come again.

❀   ❀   ❀

By noon, Lily had finished her other chores and headed into the apothecary. Other than the forest, this was her favorite place to be. The tangy and sometimes sweet and spicy smell of the herbs circled around her as she moved about the room. A whiff of mint, then the full scent of rose petals . . .

Lily began chopping, peeling, and boiling the herbs.

Some she ground into powders for brews, some she hung to dry from the rafters, while others she soaked in spirits.

She was sniffing fennel roots that had spoiled when the door burst open. Startled, Lily threw up her hands, scattering roots and leaves on the floor.

A bedraggled figure lurched in.

"Mother!" Lily cried.

"A woman," Allyce wailed. Her cloak and bliaut soaking wet, she leaned against the wall, one hand braced to keep her steady. With eyes tightly shut, she swayed. Her hair fell loose from its coils, clinging in curves to her thin cheeks. " 'Twas a woman we hung today."

"A woman? Nay!" Lily could easily imagine the evil men who were sentenced to die, but a woman? "Why?"

"She stole candles from the Church."

Lily knew it was a dreadful sin to steal from the Church, but they were only candles. Was a bit of animal fat or beeswax worth a woman's life? Is that what her mother had meant by judging too harshly?

"A woman," Allyce moaned. "Near my age!" She said no more, but hung her head.

Lily held back a moment, then she stepped close and

encircled her mother in her arms. The wet clothes quickly soaked through Lily's tunic, but she barely noticed. Her mother shook with sorrow as Lily stroked her wet hair.

A long while later, when her mother's sobs turned to shivers, Lily led her before the fire and stripped off her clothes. Then she wrapped her in blankets and pulled her bed close to the fire and lay her down gently.

Allyce's breathing finally settled to a raspy burr. Lily stared into the fire. She imagined the thief— the woman—standing on the platform, her hands tied behind her back, the man with the black hood wrapping the heavy noose around her neck, then pulling on the rope until the tips of her toes quivered in the air.

"She sinned against God," Lily said fiercely to the fire. "She had to die."

The fire did not reply, and the jumping and dancing flames lulled Lily to sleep. She awoke much later to the sound of thumping boots entering the cottage. When she opened her eyes, she froze in terror, seeing a tall man wearing a black hood and black gloves. Then he stepped into the firelight and she weakened with relief. It was not the executioner from her dreams, but only her father with a cloak pulled over his head against the rain, and a trick of the light.

❧   ❧   ❧

Like a thief, the fever came in the night.

After her father had come home and started drinking, Lily had fallen asleep on the rush mat next to her mother's bed.

It was her mother's shallow breathing that awoke Lily. At first she thought the shushing sound was her father tying together bundles of rushes to fix the roof, but the noise was too even and close. She glanced at her mother and noticed, even in the dim light, that her face burned red. Lily jerked up and placed a hand against her mother's forehead. Hot. Far too hot.

She ran into the apothecary, nearly tripping over her father on the other side of the leather curtain. An empty jug lay beside him. She shook his shoulder.

"Wake up, Father. Wake up!"

Will snorted as if coming close to waking, then he turned his head away from her and snored.

"Father!" She shook him harder.

"Be gone," he grumbled without opening his eyes.

"Mother has a fever. She needs you!" Lily waited for a reply, but all she got was another deep snore. "Too much to drink," she said with disgust, standing and kicking her father's leg harder than she meant to, but he didn't stir.

Lily pulled aside the curtain that separated the cottage from the apothecary, and held it open by draping it over a wooden peg in the wall. This way she could gather the medicines in the smaller room, while still keeping watch over her mother.

Her hands shook. Why did her father have to drink so much last night? What if she gave her mother the wrong medicine and made the fever worse?

Trying to clear her mind of her horrible thoughts, she stood before the apothecary table and looked down at the herbs and plants and boxes of grains and seeds, and at the flasks of tinctures and concoctions. She reached for some celandine to make a tincture and wondered whether a hot poultice of mint on her mother's chest would do any good for the cough. Trying not to twist her thoughts into worry knots, she worked quickly. She placed a pot of water over the fire, and when it came to a boil she poured the steaming liquid into a cup with crushed white willow bark, making a brew to help reduce the fever. She also made a mixture of borage and set it aside.

Taking the cup with the willow brew, Lily knelt beside her mother's mattress. Gently, she raised Allyce's head with one hand and held the cup to her cracked lips with the other. She dribbled the liquid into her mother's mouth. More spilled down her chin and neck than was swallowed, but Lily hoped any little bit would help.

For what seemed like hours, Lily moved ceaselessly back and forth between the apothecary and the cottage, stepping over her father and occasionally stopping to give him a good shake or a swift kick in hopes that he would awaken. He slept on while Lily racked her memory for infusions or powders that might cool her mother's fever.

At last, exhausted in body and ideas, she knelt beside her mother.

Allyce coughed weakly and her eyes fluttered open.

"I'm here, Mother," Lily said, bending forward and smiling with relief.

"Lily," her mother said, her voice barely a whisper. A fit of weak coughing followed.

Lily lifted her mother to a sitting position, supporting Allyce's back and head with her arm. She didn't notice her father until he spoke.

"What are you doing?" he hollered, stumbling into the room.

"I'm caring for Mother!" Anger rose in Lily's voice. "While you slept off your ale, I nursed Mother. She burns with fever and she is too weak to cough as strongly as she should."

"Why didn't you awaken me?" her father demanded.

"Find the bruises on your leg," Lily retorted, "and you'll know that I tried." Lily had never before spoken to her father like this, and she half expected a thrashing, but he simply knelt beside Allyce and took her hand out of Lily's.

"My Allyce," he said in a voice Lily hadn't heard in a long while. "Gentle Allyce, what ails you?"

Lily blinked with surprise. Her parents rarely passed harsh words to each other, but neither did they speak sweetly as her father did now. At least not when Lily was around to hear it.

" 'Tis just a bit of fever," Allyce whispered in a breathy voice. "Yesterday's rain . . ."

Will smoothed a large hand over his wife's forehead. "Hush. I'll prepare some comfrey and willow tea. Just rest."

"Father, I gave her some while you slept," Lily said,

stung that he would think she hadn't already done all she could for her mother. She went on to list what she gave.

Her father nodded. "You've done well."

Lily sagged with relief, glad her father was finally awake. Surely he could cure her mother. "What can we do now?"

Will uncovered a sharp instrument from a shelf in the apothecary. Lily recognized it right away, though she had only seen this procedure done once when she had secretly watched her parents tend to a patient.

"We need to balance her humors," he said.

Lily named the four humors silently: choler, phlegm, black bile, and blood. She knew that if they were not in perfect balance, any number of maladies could attack a person. Bloodletting would help realign them so her mother would get well.

Her father stretched Allyce's arm out to the side. Lily saw blue veins, like rivers, running down the length of her arm. Will chose one of the veins and cut into it. Blood poured from the incision. Lily held a cup to collect it.

As time passed, her mother grew weaker, but her cough subsided and she seemed to rest easier.

" 'Tis working, I think," Lily whispered.

Her father nodded solemnly. "We'll bleed her a little more to be sure. Go prepare a bit of self-heal to mend the wound."

Lily let her father take the cup of blood while she prepared the poultice, which would act as a styptic to stop the bleeding. She finished quickly so she could return and be by her mother's side.

Her father applied the poultice, wrapping Allyce's arm tightly with a strip of cloth.

Lily felt her mother's forehead. "She's still warm."

"She's sleeping now," Will replied, "but the bleeding will help her."

Lily nodded firmly, as if by agreeing and believing it would make it so.

❧ ❧ ❧

They sat with Allyce all night. Though she tried not to, Lily dozed off and slept fitfully. Every time she jerked awake, she found her father feeding her mother or talking to her in a low voice.

At last dawn crept into the tiny cottage. With eyes that itched from lack of sleep, Lily tended her morning chores while her father remained at Allyce's side.

Blossom scratched at the door a long while before giving up. Lily wanted to play with her dog and walk through the forest to relieve the cramps of sitting in one place for so long, but she felt ashamed for even thinking of leaving her mother's side.

That afternoon when the sun was high, her mother opened her eyes and smiled. It was all Lily could do to keep from bursting with joy.

Allyce tried to talk, but Will hushed her. "Save your strength, dear wife," he said soothingly.

Lily leaned over and kissed her mother's cheek. Then she flew outside, calling for Blossom. The dog appeared from behind a pile of firewood, wagging her stubby tail.

"Come along," Lily called, running into the forest. "Mother's going to be just fine."

❧   ❧   ❧

A sennight passed. During those seven days and nights, Lily helped her father with the medicines, since her mother was still too weak to rise. Allyce still lay by the hearth, though she said she felt stronger every day. Secretly, Lily didn't think she looked any stronger. But she was afraid to voice her fears.

Some afternoons, Lily found John waiting for her outside by the cages. She came to expect him, and when he didn't come, she missed his company.

One day, she found the boy sniffling and curled up under a willow. Blossom nudged him with her cold nose, and even that didn't make John smile.

Lily crouched next to him and tentatively lay a hand on the back of his shoulder.

When he looked up, she saw a purple bruise around his eye and a long, shallow cut on his cheek. "What happened?" she exclaimed.

"I left the flour keg open. The rats came and feasted," he said bleakly.

Lily groaned. "Was it all ruined?"

"Most of it. And Mum said 'twas especially disgraceful because I'm to be Master Miller's apprentice soon, and if the miller hears of this, he may not want to take me on."

Lily sat next to him. "Does your father beat you often?" she asked gently.

He looked at her sideways, his injured eye nearly puffed closed. " 'Twas my mum who did this."

Lily couldn't imagine her mother hitting her, or even her father, though she was sure she'd deserved it a time or two. "Does it hurt?"

"Nay," he said, but she could see from the streaks of dried tears on his cheeks that he was trying to be brave.

A few weeks ago, she might have taunted him about the tears. But it was different now.

Lily jumped to her feet. "I'll be back in a moment." She crept into the apothecary and took what she'd need for John's injuries. Her parents, sitting in the cottage by the crackling fire, didn't hear her. Under the willow tree again, the trailing branches hiding them from sight, Lily cleaned John's wound with wine, then applied a poultice.

John wrinkled his nose. "What's in it?" he asked.

Lily laughed and told him the contents. He didn't seem too impressed by her knowledge of herbs and got up soon after to leave. But before he left, he looked at her shyly through his one good eye.

"It feels better already," he admitted. "Thank you."

Lily waved her hand at him, feeling a blush creep into her cheeks. "Be gone, John the brave," she said, pretending irritation. "I have no more time for you."

He grinned at her, his puffy eye looking painfully squeezed. With a slight nod in her direction, he took off.

Lily lay back and smiled up at the tree branches. She had helped her mother get well and now John. Perhaps someday she would be a real healer like her parents.

She blew a strand of hair off her forehead. *A healer and an executioner's assistant,* she corrected herself. She knew one did not necessarily have to come with the other, except in her case it did, and there was no escaping it.

CHAPTER FIVE

Her mother's recovery was slow. Even after a fortnight, she still complained of a constant pain in her side, and her breathing became labored if she did more than stand. But Lily's father assured her that all was going as well as could be expected.

Every day, Lily checked on her animals, letting go a few of the rabbits, only to capture one of them a few hours later that had barely escaped the claws of a falcon. Then the day finally came to release the fox.

Lily crouched beside the collection of cages. The kit ran in circles with excitement. "Aye," she said to the animal, "today you are going free. And the rest of you, too, as soon as you are strong enough to run away from hunters with arrows and boys with sharp sticks. And birds of prey," she added for her reinjured friend.

After tying up Blossom, she fed the animals and examined their healing wounds, then she took a long length of rope to the fox's cage. Opening the small door, she blocked the exit so the creature couldn't run out and disappear into the surrounding forest. Lily wanted to lead the fox far away from town, where, hopefully, he would find a family of his own.

Once the rope was tied around the fox's neck, she pulled the reluctant animal out of his cage. He balked, straightening his forelegs and twisting his head back and forth to rid himself of the rope.

"Come on, stubborn kit," Lily said, relaxing the tension on the lead. "You can't stay here forever."

With the rope slackened, the fox took a tentative step out of the cage. Then another. Soon he was trotting beside Lily, just as long as she didn't pull on the rope. When she did, he stiffened his legs and Lily had to drag him. She put up with this for a while, but finally she scooped the kit into her arms, where he settled quite comfortably.

"We'll never get far enough away with you dawdling and me dragging you," Lily said, picking up her pace. As she walked, she scratched behind the fox's large ears and hummed the songs her mother used to sing to her as a child.

Suddenly she stopped and turned. "I see you, John the tailor's son," she called to the small figure behind the tree. "I know you're there," Lily said, tapping her foot. "You want to see where I leave this poor animal so you can catch him with your pointy stick," she teased. By now she knew very well that John loved the animals almost as much as she did.

"Nay," the shadow said, finally pulling away from the tree. John came closer. "He's too handsome to kill."

"Oh, so the rabbit you near speared wasn't handsome enough to let live?"

"I can eat a rabbit," John said stubbornly. "Besides, I haven't hunted with the others for a long while."

"True," Lily agreed.

They walked the rest of the morning side by side. Lily glanced at his eye and was pleased to see it had healed nicely.

When they came to a small clearing, Lily put the fox down and untied the rope.

"This will be your new home," she said.

The fox scuttled off, sniffing the ground. Soon, even the white tip of his tail was lost from sight in the tall meadow grass. He was healed and free, but he had run away without saying goodbye. She remembered helping her mother tend his wounds, and staying up with him the first few nights as he lay on a rush nest she had made for him next to her own pallet. Just then his nose poked out of the grass and he yipped. Lily laughed. He said goodbye after all.

❧   ❧   ❧

John headed off on his own when they neared the town walls.

"Come see Blossom," Lily called after him. "She's getting fatter every day."

He waved without looking back.

At home, much was the same. Her mother rested before the fire, while her father sat on a bench whittling a spoon, his eyes rarely leaving his wife.

Lily set about making supper. She and her father ate roasted chicken and leftover mutton pie. Allyce ate next to nothing.

After the meal, Lily started to clean up when she heard a familiar sound coming from outside the cottage. She gasped. It couldn't be.

She ran to the window and peered out. Indeed it was! She raced out the door, her father calling after her, "What is it?"

Lily gave her answer by returning with a bundle of red fur in her arms. Her kit had come back to her. She knelt beside her mother. "Look who followed me home," she said. She couldn't help the smile that curled her lips.

Her mother shook her head. "This is not his home."

"But he likes it here. Why can't I keep him?"

"Blossom will tear him to shreds as soon as you untie her."

Lily frowned. That was true. Though her dog was sweet and dear to her, she was a hunter. "I could keep him in a cage." But even as she said the words, she knew how wrong they were. All creatures deserved to be free.

"What can I do?" she said. "I took him far away this morning."

"The kit loves you, so you must make him hate you," her mother said.

"What do you mean?"

Allyce paused for a bit, catching her breath. "You must scare him away. Chase him. Throw rocks at him if you must."

"Nay! I could never do that."

"If you love him, you must set him free even if it tears you apart," Allyce said. She closed her eyes as though the conversation were too much for her.

Will put a heavy hand on Lily's shoulder, shaking his head to silence her. "Put him in a cage for tonight. You can set the fox free tomorrow."

ॐ ॐ ॐ

The next morning, Lily went about churning the goat's milk and making dough. She swept the hearth, brought in a new pile of wood for the fire, then scrubbed the largest of the kettles.

"Lily?"

Lily dashed to her mother's side. "What is it? Are you chilled?"

With a weak smile, her mother waved away her words. "What are you doing?"

Lily sat back on her heels. "I'm doing my chores."

"You're stalling," Allyce said.

Lily bit her lip. "But there's so much to do . . ."

"Go," Allyce said. "Take the kit where he belongs. 'Tis what you must do."

Lily sighed. With one last pleading look, which only got her another wave of her mother's hand, she went outside to the cages. She took the young fox in her arms, as she had the last time, and made her way through the forest, taking care to stay off any paths. The closer she got to the clearing, the slower she walked. The light from the clearing became brighter and brighter, as though the sun shone down only on this small patch of land and nowhere else. And no matter how much she dragged her feet, she came at last to the edge of the small meadow.

Lily rubbed her cheek against the kit's head and he nudged her with his nose. Laughing sadly, she set him down. This time he didn't bound off into the tall grass; he sniffed around her shoes, scooting under her skirts and winding between her legs.

"Go on," Lily said. "Be off with you." Gently she nudged the animal away with one foot. "No, fool, I'm not playing. Go away. This is your home now."

The little fox tilted his head and looked up at her.

Gritting her teeth, Lily pulled a stone out of the sack she had tied around her waist. "Please go," she begged. Then she shouted, "Go! Leave!" The fox jumped away from her. Lily threw the rock, and then another, and again and again until her sack was empty and the bushy tail of the fox was nowhere to be seen.

With an aching heart, Lily ran back into the woods, feeling as though she'd just smashed her soul into pieces.

"I cannot!" Lily exclaimed the next day.

"You must," her father replied.

From her bed, Allyce said softly, "You can, child. You went with me every year, and now you will go alone."

"But all those people," Lily said, "they'll taunt me."

"You'll wear a cloak and hood to shade your face as we always do," her mother interrupted. "No one will look too closely."

Lily stared beseechingly at her father. "Can't you go?"

Will shook his head firmly. "Lord Dunsworth has called for me. I must go to the castle."

Lily turned to her mother, but one look at Allyce's frail countenance stopped her tongue. She couldn't ask her mother to come with her, not when it was still such an effort for her to simply sit up.

Lily bit her lip. She could see her parents were firm on this. She must go to the town fair and buy goods. Her father had already listed the needed items, among them wool cloth, leather for boots and pouches, and secretly he'd told her to get a ribbon for her mother's hair. Something to help cheer her.

Lily put on her cloak and pulled a hood over her head. Taking a deep breath, she stooped next to her mother and tried to smile bravely.

"I go now," she said, trying to sound confident. She didn't want her mother worrying about her while she was gone.

Her mother stroked Lily's cheek. "All will be well," she assured her.

Lily placed her hand over her mother's even though terror coiled in her stomach. She stood up and turned quickly to the door. Her father nodded to her as she left.

The autumn air swirled briskly through the trees and clouds scuttled across the sky, piling up on the eastern horizon. Lily was glad for the cloak for more than one reason. She decided to take a different path toward town so that she'd have a better chance of arriving unrecognized. She could blend in with the others attending the fair and, with any luck, no one would know who she was.

Farmers and travelers from nearby towns made their way through the gates. There was much gaiety as friends and families reunited after many months since the last fair. This was a time for laughter and games and goodwill toward all. *Toward all except me,* Lily thought, burrowing deeper into her cloak.

She walked quickly, keeping her face down. The dirty, winding streets finally led her to the center of town, where the merchants had set up colorful tents to display their wares. Jugglers wended through the crowds, making people laugh. A group of musicians played while the audience finished off a bawdy ditty.

Not far from the musicians, Lily had to skirt a large crowd. She couldn't see what was going on, and she didn't care to, she told herself. She would do her errands quickly as she and her mother always had, and then she'd hurry home to where she belonged.

Lily came across the wool merchant first, where she bought a length of soft wool. Then she followed the stench of newly tanned leather to the leather seller, where she bought enough for three new pairs of boots. Nearby, she picked up some tallow candles and at the tinker's she bought a small pan her father needed.

Once she was loaded down with goods, she carried them in a sack under her cloak. Lily was intent on leaving, but along the way, the scent of baking pies distracted her. Her father had given her a spare coin from their meager allotment, as though he'd known she'd be tempted by some mulled cider or a piece of gingerbread. It all smelled delicious. Lily walked back and forth between the many stalls selling food and drinks, trying to decide what to buy.

"Lily?" a hoarse whisper said.

A lump of dread weighted her stomach. She had been recognized.

CHAPTER SIX

Lily stood as still as a tombstone. She didn't know if it would be better to run or hide.

"Lily," the voice said again.

Without moving her head, Lily looked around, her gaze finally falling on John standing near her. Relief loosened her clenched hands.

The boy moved closer and looked up, giving Lily half a smile. "What are you doing here?"

She glanced around to make sure no one was watching them, then she quickly showed him the sack that held her purchases. "Now go away before you draw attention to me," she said.

"Nay, I'm allowed to be here same as you." He scowled at her. "Besides, I'm here to buy some gingerbread. Only I think the cakes over yonder look fine, too."

"Cakes?" Lily said. Then she bit her tongue for sounding interested.

John grinned. "Aye, with sugar and cinnamon and whole nuts and—" He licked his lips. "Come on, I'll show you."

Reluctantly, Lily found herself following the small boy. But before they got to the cake seller, their path was blocked by a large crowd. John jerked his head for Lily to stay close as they threaded their way through the people. She'd never felt such a press of bodies. It was both frightening and exhilarating. A bit guiltily, she thought of the people's reaction if they realized who was pushing by them. They would not be pleased to find themselves so close to her.

Before she knew it, she was in the center of the crowd, staring up at a large bear dancing on his hind legs. An iron cuff circled his neck and a long, thick chain was attached to it and held by a man dressed in crimson and green.

Lily glanced around at the laughing people, wondering what humor they saw in a shackled bear. She longed to set it free.

"Come on," John said, tugging on her cloak. "The tumblers are this way. You'll like them better." He led her back out through the crowd and to another group of people who were clapping and cheering as boys dressed in tight leggings climbed on each other's shoulders and tossed each other through the air.

Lily marveled at their performance. When the misty rain blew in, she barely noticed. When the rain fell harder, the tumblers bowed and the crowd dispersed. With no more to distract them, Lily and John tramped from one stall to the next, trying to decide what treat to buy. She finally settled on a warm piece of cake, which she ate in the pelting rain, laughing when it got so soggy that she had to shove nearly half of it into her mouth before it fell apart. John laughed, too, huddling his nose and hands over a cup of hot cider, the steam blowing in his eyes. For a moment she forgot who she was.

"John!" someone called.

The boy jerked his head up. His face turned red, and without even a glance at Lily, he hurried toward his pack of friends. Lily recognized them as the boys with the pointy sticks. They talked to John and he shrugged uneasily. One of them gestured toward Lily, and she turned away, dread replacing happiness. Rain seeped through her cloak and muddy water oozed into her worn shoes.

Sloshing through the puddles, she reached the edge

of the fair before she remembered one last item she had yet to get. How could she have forgotten the ribbon for her mother's hair? She should be home tending to her instead of out playing in the rain.

Quickly she found a woman selling brightly dyed ribbons. Lily chose a deep blue color to match her mother's eyes. She tucked the ribbon under her cloak as she hurried through town and out the gates, taking the shortest path home.

Her hood fell back and the driving rain stung her cheeks as she ran. Lily burst into the cottage with so much on her mind, so much to tell her mother!

Allyce was not on her bed.

Lily hastily threw off her cloak and dropped her purchases on the floor. "Mother!" she cried. "Mother!"

No one answered.

She ran into the apothecary. Her mother lay next to the table, one arm stretched out as though she had been reaching for something. A quick glance told Lily that her mother had been preparing a concoction when exhaustion must have overtaken her and she'd fallen.

Lily bent down and put her arms around Allyce, noticing that her mother's clothes felt damp. She half lifted her mother, half dragged her back to the bed and laid her there, piling blankets on top of her. Lily stoked the dying fire and added logs until it raged fiercely, but not as fiercely as the guilt that burned inside her.

❧   ❧   ❧

Many hours later, Lily lay on her own pallet behind her curtain. Her father had come home, only to find Allyce burning with fever once again.

In silence, he had bled Allyce and fixed a dozen remedies for her, but her fever stayed high, and she moaned and twisted.

Lily was unable to sleep. Afraid to sleep. Afraid of what she might wake to. Eventually her eyes closed against her will. When she opened them again, the storm was gone and the sunlight spread through the cottage like a widening puddle.

Her father sat on a stool, staring down at his wife. Lily's breath caught in her throat until she saw the faint up and down of her mother's chest. She was still alive! Lily scrambled out of bed and hurried to her side, eager to apologize for taking so long at the fair. But her mother didn't even stir when Lily took her hand and kissed it.

"Lily," her father began.

She shook her head. She didn't want her father to tell her what she knew deep in her soul.

She and her father sat beside her mother for hours. They did not speak or eat. They simply waited.

❧ ❧ ❧

The end came peacefully for Allyce, though it tore Lily apart. The tears she had buried for so long bubbled to the surface. They came soft at first, like a gentle rain. Then she cried as hard as she could, wishing her tears would wash the pain away, but they did nothing more than dampen the front of her dress.

Lily looked at her father. He sat as still as stone, and his eyes were dry. "Don't you care?" she asked through her tears.

He turned to her, his gaze bleak and dark. "Far too much," he said in a hoarse voice.

Lily wondered if he had buried his tears the way she had. And perhaps by now he had forgotten how to cry.

She went to him and put her arms about his broad shoulders and cradled his head against her neck.

"Why did she leave us?" Lily asked. "Is it because we are cursed as everyone says?"

He embraced her. "Everyone must die. 'Tis our fate, child."

Lily bowed her head in defeat. One could not argue with fate.

❧   ❧   ❧

Because she was the executioner's wife, Allyce was not allowed to be buried in the churchyard, or even have a service and funeral procession. Besides, Lily thought bitterly, who but herself and her father would be there to mourn her?

Together, Lily and Will prepared Allyce for burial and carried her into the forest. Will dug a grave. They set the body in the hole, and before they covered it with dirt, Lily lay a dove's feather on her mother's breast.

"You are free now," she whispered, then she dropped the first clods of earth into the grave.

In silence, her father packed the ground until there was only a slight mound to show where Allyce was buried. He left, and when he came back he struggled to carry a large stone, which he dropped at the head of the grave. He turned it carefully.

Lily saw the words her father had carved under a crooked cross.

Allyce
Mother
Wife

But what of healer? And friend? And comforter? How could an entire life be reduced to a name and two words? She bowed her head, longing for her mother's soft voice. For gentle arms to hold her.

A heavy hand pressed down on her shoulder and she turned against her father's chest. His arms were hard and unyielding, but they circled her like the walls around the town, offering protection. She gratefully accepted what she could get. Lily squeezed her eyes shut to stop the tears. The time for crying had passed.

✖ ✖ ✖

During October, days blew in brisk, taking with them the leaves on the trees and any warmth left in the sun, and nights were cold. Lily barely noticed. She worked in the apothecary beside her father, determined to learn all the secrets of healing. She already knew much, but her father knew far more. And yet it hadn't been enough.

It wasn't her father's fault Allyce had died, as her fate had determined she should. But if she had died according to her destiny, then what had her mother meant when she'd said she'd cheated fate? How had her father saved Allyce from her fate? Had he healed her in some way?

Lily longed to ask, but her father kept himself tightly shuttered. He worked endlessly, as though he, too, were obsessed with discovering what healing draught or poultice he could have used to save his wife. At night he did not drink heavily as he did after an execution or after a day working in Lord Dunsworth's dungeon. Instead, he sat silent, staring into the fire, or he went outside and chopped far more wood than they would need in three winters.

One morning, John appeared beside the cages while Lily was tending to the animals. Lily smiled widely. "John the miller's apprentice!"

The boy returned a shy smile as though they were strangers.

Good as, Lily thought. He hadn't come around in several weeks.

As if hearing her thoughts, he said, "Master Miller has kept me busy from sunup till sundown."

"And now you can grind wheat into flour like a master?"

He scowled. "Nay. All I do is sweep!"

Lily threw back her head and laughed. After long weeks of solemn concentration in the apothecary, it felt wonderful. John's scowl turned into a grin and he laughed, too. Only then did Lily realize he held a bundle of rags close to his stomach.

He noticed her looking and handed it to her. "My brother caught it yesterday and broke its wing. He wanted to keep it so it couldn't fly away. But it hasn't eaten or had a drop to drink since then."

Lily unwrapped the rags to find a soft gray dove. Suddenly her eyes burned. She blinked to hold back the tears. Doves would always remind her of her mother.

"I was going to wring its neck," John continued.

"Nay!"

"To keep it from dying slowly," he said hurriedly. "But then I thought to bring it to you."

Lily nodded. " 'Tis well you did. Come." She headed into the apothecary.

John peered through the dark doorway. "Is your father home?" he whispered.

"Nay, he's at the castle and he won't be home till dark."

John entered and she handed him the bird. Then she cleared a place on the trestle table and gathered what she thought she'd need to set the wing and wrap it so it would mend. Before she started, she felt a pang of fear. If only her mother were here to show her the proper way to hold the bird and calm it.

Once again she took the bird from John. "Help me hold it," she said softly, so as not to startle the dove.

After only a second's hesitation, he moved close to her and did as she asked. She worked quickly and carefully until the wing was folded against the bird's body and bandaged firmly in place.

"Will it be able to fly again?" John asked as they took the bird outside to a cage.

Lily didn't want to tell him how unsure she was. How she missed her mother's advice in caring for her animals. She had never attempted to mend a broken wing, and she could only pray that she had done well. But to John she said, "Aye."

John smiled. "Then I'm glad I did not wring its pretty little neck." Lily took a swipe at him, but he ducked away, laughing. He looked at the sky. "I'm late. The miller will take the broom to my backside if I don't hurry." He turned to go, but at the last moment stopped and faced Lily. "I heard about your mum, and I'm sorry."

Lily nodded, not daring to speak for fear her voice would crack.

With a wave, John left.

❧   ❧   ❧

Mid-afternoon, a sennight later, Blossom whined from the corner of the cottage farthest away from the hearth. The dog had pulled the blanket off Lily's pallet and now lay on it, panting heavily.

"At last!" Lily exclaimed. She sat down on the rush mat and leaned forward. Blossom whimpered up at her. "Good girl," Lily crooned, scratching the dog behind the ears.

She watched as Blossom gave birth to four spotted pups. Three of them were plump; one was small and looked more like a mouse. Blossom licked them all clean. The larger pups snuggled up to Blossom's belly for their first meal, but the runt couldn't even lift his head. Lily tried to prod him forward toward a teat, but once he got there, the puppy didn't seem to know what to do. Besides, the others quickly pushed him out of the way.

Lily dug through a chest in the apothecary and found the nipple made of sheep's intestines she had used to nurse a fawn earlier in the year. It was too large for the pup, but with some string and careful cutting, she was able to make it a bit smaller. It would do for now, she decided. Later she could make smaller ones.

She wiped off the fat they had used to keep the nipple supple, then she mixed a bit of goat's milk with water. Filling a small leather pouch, she attached the nipple with some twine.

Sitting next to Blossom so that the dog wouldn't think she was stealing one of her pups, Lily picked up the runt and cradled the tiny creature in her left hand. She dribbled some milk against his lips. After a bit, the pup licked the milk away.

An hour later, Lily's back was stiff and her shoulders sore from sitting in one position for so long. Finally full, a dribble at a time, the pup was asleep. She kissed him on the nose, then lay him next to his family.

When her father came home from town, Lily showed him the pups. He admired them solemnly. He seemed to be thinking on something else. Ever since her mother died, her father seemed more distant and preoccupied. She knew well that he loved her, but she also knew not to expect any hearty laughter or wide smiles.

"There are four, just as you said there would be," Will said.

"I dreamed it."

The words startled them both. Lily's heart thumped, though she didn't know if it was out of fear or joy.

Her father peered at her intently. "Do you dream as your mother did?"

"Aye," she said, suddenly realizing it was true. "I've dreamed a few dreams. But I had forgotten them until now."

Her father took her hand. "You are so much like your mother." He stared deeply into her eyes, she felt he must be looking right through her, searching for the wife he had lost. "I thank God I still have you."

Surprised at the thick emotion in her father's voice, she said, "And I, you."

He shook his head, as though to rid himself of a trance.

Lily slipped her hand from his and set the table. As she worked, she couldn't stop thinking about her mother's dreams, and she wondered if she would start having more of them. Would hers be like the tales her mother often had? Or would they be practical like how many pups Blossom would bear? Or would they be the kind her mother didn't like to talk about?

ജ   ജ   ജ

Through early November, Lily spent her evenings stitching the hem of the cloak her mother had promised her. It was made from the wool cloth she'd purchased at the fair. When the light coming in through the window became too dim, she put away her sewing and prepared dinner. She wasn't a very good cook, but her father never complained about the soups or stews she put before him. And when the bread came out flat or burnt, he didn't say a word of reproach.

One night before supper, her father came in from the apothecary and sat on the bench. He leaned his elbows on the table and blew out a breath.

"I think the runt will live," Lily commented.

"Aye."

"He takes the nipple well and has grown a bit, don't you think?"

Will nodded.

Lily narrowed her eyes at her father. "Gained two or three stone, I should think," she said, purposely exaggerating.

He nodded again.

Lily knocked the wooden spoon on the edge of the pot. "You're not even listening to me."

He shrugged absently, his left shoulder rising higher as it always did. Saying nothing, he simply sat there, his head tilted, his eyes staring into the flame of a candle.

Lily turned back to the fire. A moment later, she heard her father heave himself to his feet and return to his apothecary without a word. Curious, she moved aside the curtain just a hair and watched him bend over the worktable. His back looked hunched with age and his lips moved as though in silent prayer. It took a moment for her to make out what he was fingering on the scarred wood surface. It was her mother's copper ring. It had always made Allyce's finger green, but her husband couldn't afford a silver one. Even so, Allyce had worn it every day simply because Will had given it to her. It was her only piece of jewelry.

Without a sound, Lily withdrew. Then she called through the curtain as if she had not been spying on him, "Come to supper, Father." She had to call three more times before he did as beckoned.

After supper, when her father usually returned to his apothecary to work, he watched Lily wipe clean the cup and spoons they had used, feed the trencher to Blossom, and pet the pups, taking extra care to kiss the runt. As she did these things, Lily shifted uneasily under his watchful eye.

Finally she turned to him. "What is it, Father? Why are you staring at me so?"

Will drew in a deep breath before he spoke. "The time has come," he began slowly, "for you to assist me in my duties."

CHAPTER SEVEN

Lily paused as her father reached beneath the bench and handed her his cloak, which he'd gathered into a bundle. She took the cloak, realizing immediately that something was hidden within its folds. A tremor of fear struck between her shoulder blades until she assured herself that it couldn't be an ax. "What's in here?"

"Open it and see."

She pulled away the heavy material, finally revealing the hidden object. "My own mortar and pestle!"

"Aye, you've learned much, these last months. 'Tis time you became my assistant . . . in all I do."

Lily barely noticed the hesitation in her father's voice. She hugged him. She would help him heal people. She would speak softly and kindly as her mother used to, and she'd touch with gentle hands instead of the clumsy ones she still faltered with.

Between her laughs, a scratch at the back door caught her attention. A night visitor could only mean one thing. Holding a candle high and hurrying to the apothecary door, Lily looked out. A young man stood there, supporting an older man with sallow cheeks. Both men had gaunt faces and their clothes were little more than rags. The older man held up his hand. Or rather, the bloody stump where his hand used to be.

Lily gasped and fell back a step, but her father's firm hand on her shoulder quickly steadied her.

" 'Tis my father," the younger man said. "He's lost much blood, and his arm is hot." He kept his gaze lowered. "We tried to care for it ourselves and even saw the barber, but we have nothing for payment and he sent us away. I didn't want to come here! But Father says 'tis his only hope."

Lily stiffened at the venom in his voice.

"Come in," Will ordered, walking back and pulling Lily with him.

The two men entered. Lily's father sat the wounded man on a bench and began to unwind the bandage that was black with blood and grime. "Heat some water, daughter," he said curtly.

She moved quickly to do his bidding, ashamed that he'd had to ask. As his assistant, she should know what to do without being told.

Once she'd placed a kettle of rainwater over the small fire, Lily helped her father lay out herbs. She tried not to look at the mutilated arm that rested on the table. But one quick glance made her stomach roil. The flesh looked painfully red with infection and the edges of the skin were pulling back from the wound. She just hoped she wouldn't faint and do her father dishonor. If she were to become a healer, she would have to tend to injuries as bad as this. Maybe even worse.

"What a terrible accident," she said, trying to fill the heavy silence.

"Aye," the injured man grunted.

"A scythe did this?" Lily asked, unable to think of any other instrument that could possibly do so much damage.

Her father's hands stilled. The old man said nothing.

Lily glanced at him. He was looking at her from under heavyset lids. His eyes appeared sunken and near death. She noticed the stiff frown on her father's face as he mixed various herbs.

Lily shifted uneasily, suddenly aware of the tension stretching thin in the room. Looking at the bloody stump as her father examined it, she wondered what kind of an accident could possibly cleave off a hand so precisely. Scything accidents did happen, but the wounds were rarely clear through nor cut so smoothly as this one. An ax perhaps?

A humming noise started in her ears. She shook her head, trying to concentrate on her duties as her father's assistant. She remembered her mother often gave kind words of advice to visitors, so she said, "You should be more careful."

The young man made a choking sound and she looked up at him, shocked to see such hatred in his eyes. He glared at her until she blinked and looked away, the heat of humiliation rising from her neck and covering her face.

The truth dawned slowly and painfully. The humming in her ears grew louder, and suddenly the candlelight wasn't bright enough. She clutched the edge of the table to keep from swaying.

She stared at the stump as her father swabbed the

wound with strong wine. Then he tried to bring the edges of the wound together, pinching the skin between his fingers. The old man squirmed, but he did not cry out in pain.

Her father started to chant. "In the name of the Father, Son, and Holy Mary. The wound was red, the cut deep, the flesh be sore, but there will be no more blood or pain till the blessed Virgin bears a child again."

Solemnly, he applied a poultice to draw out any infection and help halt the bleeding. He also prepared several decoctions for the older man, and another poultice to take away with him.

The father and son left without another word. On unsteady legs, Lily followed them and closed the door at their backs. Turning, she leaned against the door frame and watched her father start to clean the table.

"Father?"

He turned to her, his face molten in the flickering light of the candles.

"Tell me what happened to his hand."

Will turned back to his work without answering right away. Finally he said, "It was cut off." His voice broke and he coughed to clear it. Then he continued. "He was caught stealing pies from Mistress Baker. Lord Dunsworth sentenced him to lose his hand for the theft."

"It was your doing."

" 'Tis my duty," he replied, his voice firm.

"But they looked half starved. Surely one pie—"

"I am not the judge nor jury. I did not write the laws." He slammed a fist on the table. "I only do as I am told! As my father did before me."

Lily jumped. Without another word, she edged out of the apothecary and into the cottage. She put on her old cloak, since the new one wasn't finished yet, and slipped out the front door. She walked through the night forest to her mother's grave.

Lily visited her mother often, keeping the grave swept and bringing flowers that had survived the frost, or feathers to lay there. She knelt beside the stone her father had carved, and bowed her head.

"Mother," Lily said softly, laying a hand on the stone. Despair washed over her. Never before had she so clearly seen her future. Her fate. "I cannot," she whispered. "I cannot be Father's assistant no matter how much I love him."

She sat in silence for a long time, imagining another future, a different fate. There were places, she'd heard, where healers cared for the sick and injured. Midwives who knew something of herbal remedies and helped bring forth new life. And fine doctors who studied at universities and cared for royalty.

Bit by bit, hope bloomed inside Lily. She did not have to be the executioner's daughter any longer. She could leave and settle someplace where no one knew her. She had been running away all her life, surely she could run one last time? Lily said good night to her mother and walked home.

Once inside the cottage, Lily stood before the hearth to warm her chilled hands, unsure of what to say. Sitting on a stool, Will stared into the flames as though he were afraid to look at his daughter. Lily walked over behind him and put her arms around his shoulders. He gripped her hands and kissed them. With a sinking heart, Lily wondered how she could ever leave him.

❦ ❦ ❦

A fortnight later, Lily's father announced, "Tomorrow they will raise a bright gallows in town."

Lily suddenly remembered the four men hanging, faces swollen, necks stretched long. And the man wearing the black mask who pulled the ropes. The man she still could not imagine as her father.

"You will come with me when I go to help build it."

Lily kept her eyes on the flour she sifted between her fingers.

"And you will come with me to the hanging the next day."

Still she uttered no words, for what could she possibly say? She had known the day would come to assist her father in more than just making medicine and attending to the sick who called for his healing powers. Often in the past two weeks she had tried to form the words to tell her father she was leaving. But each time, love and guilt had tied her tongue. The love between them was like a string, tangling them together in a way she could never pick apart. Or so it seemed.

Lily made a pile of the flour, then scooped out an indentation on the top where she would add the eggs, yeast, fat, water, and scant amount of salt to mix into dough. As she worked, the pups, now brave and curious, tumbled over her feet, licking her toes and tugging on the hem of her tunic. Lily nudged them gently away.

CHAPTER EIGHT

The next morning, when they passed through the gate into town, Lord Dunsworth's men stood aside. Lily didn't look at them. She kept her eyes lowered as her mother had told her to do. She followed her father along the winding roads. People took to the wall when they approached, so they were forced to walk down the middle where everyone threw their waste. She tried to step high to avoid a shoe full of filth, but it was useless. And the stench was horrible after a few warm days in late November and surprising little rain. Pigs that had gotten loose snuffled through the slop, squealing with surprise when someone kicked them out of the way.

In the center of town, a crowd had gathered to watch the gallows being raised. The men had returned with fresh pine. They stripped off the bark, leaving the wood bare and bright, so that none of the demons could hide under the bark after the thief was hanged.

The whole town helped raise the gallows. The executioner, though powerful with his ax, could not build it himself. The townsfolk believed that if everyone helped, even by pounding in a single nail, none of the blame could be placed on any one person. Therefore, the condemned man couldn't exact retribution from the other side of death. Only the executioner would have blood on his hands.

Minstrels sang and played lutes and double flutes, dancing through the crowd to the beat of a ringing tambourine. After the raising, the townsfolk would have a celebration, to which almost all were invited.

Lily stood off to one side as the men nailed and roped the gallows into place. The crowd left a wide circle around her. Children ran to and fro, and soon she caught sight of a familiar face.

"John!" she called without thinking.

The boy jerked to a stop. He started to raise his hand, but lowered it quickly as a group of older boys clustered around him, waving their arms in her direction and prodding him in the stomach. The tallest boy pushed John, and he teetered. Then another pushed him from behind and he lost his balance, falling to his knees on the cobblestones. Lily wanted to run and help him, but the look on his red face as he stood stopped her.

She hastily dropped her gaze to the ground. Even looking at the dirt on her shoes, Lily could see the children gathering around her, tightening the circle like a noose.

"Lily, Lily White as Bones," one chanted.

"Gallows Girl! Gallows Girl!"

"Don't let her look at you or she'll give you the evil eye."

Before Lily had a chance to move, something struck the side of her head. The stink of rotten egg filled the air. She looked up fiercely. The children scampered away with nervous giggles. But when Lily didn't strike them down with her glare, they crept closer. John stood off to the side, not three lengths away, with wide eyes. Someone handed him an egg.

"Go on," his friends urged. "Or are you afraid of her?"

Lily couldn't look away. She watched John slowly lift his arm and heave the egg. It hit her on the right shoulder and the impact made her flinch. The children laughed and clapped.

"Stinky Lily!" they shouted. Even John joined in the shouting and clapping.

The laughing crowd spread out wider. Lily didn't move. Not even to touch her hair where the eggs had left a sticky mess. Instead, she pretended she was a statue made of debarked pine, and the tears threatening to fall from her eyes weren't tears at all, but simply sap, flowing from the timber.

The taunting suddenly stopped. Lily jerked at a touch on her shoulder, but it was only her father.

"Go on home," he said gently.

Lily didn't want his pity. It was all his fault that this had happened. Without a word, she turned and ran.

By the time Lily got home, the egg in her hair and on her cloak had dried, but the stench still lingered. She heated some water and, using her mother's strong soap, Lily cleaned her cloak and washed her hair over and over again. Afterward, she sat before the fire, running a comb through the strands. When her father came home, Lily refused to look at him. He called to her but when she didn't answer, he shuffled into his apothecary without another word.

Lily combed her hair until it was dry, then draped her old cloak about her shoulders and went outside to check the animals. Blossom and her pups yipped along behind her.

She attended to the rabbits first, trying to concentrate on what she was doing, rather than thinking about what had just happened in town. Now there were only two rabbits left. All the rest had been let go. A hedgehog fussed as she examined the stub where a foot had been bit off by a larger animal. She was just about to check the dove, when someone called to her.

She paused, but didn't turn. She would know John the traitor's voice anywhere.

"I'm sorry, Lily," he said. His voice quavered. "I didn't want to throw the egg."

"Then why did you?" she asked, still keeping her back to him.

"I—I had to. They made me do it."

"I didn't see them holding a hot brand to you, or twisting your arm," she said bitterly.

For a moment, Lily thought the boy had deserted her, but then she heard the catch in his breath as though he were trying not to cry.

"If I didn't, they said they wouldn't play with me."

"They don't play with you now," Lily said. "They only tease you and make you do things you don't want to do." She stood up and faced him. "I thought I was your friend!"

"You are, but it would be a great dishonor to my family if anyone knew. My mother would beat me."

The words felt like slaps. "Then go away. You're not welcome here. And don't ever come back!" She chased him to the edge of the path.

"Lily . . ."

"Be gone!" She picked up a stone and threw it at him, then bent to pick up another.

John backed off down the path. "But I don't care anymore what they say. I swear it. I don't care what they say about your father, or about your mother being saved from the noose, or even about—"

The stone left Lily's hand before she even knew she had released it. It thunked against a tree trunk right next to John's head. He took off running.

"Wait!" she called after him. "What did you say?" But it was too late. He was gone.

What had John said? What had he meant?

Lily charged into the cottage, slamming the door behind her. "Father!" she called. Lily careened into the apothecary, nearly swiping the leather curtain from its hold above the doorway. "Father!"

He held up a hand to stall her. "Fifteen, sixteen, seventeen . . ." he counted as drops of liquid dripped from a wooden spoon into a flask.

"Father!" She pulled the flask away from him. The liquid splashed out of the container. "What did he mean? What did he mean about Mother? What noose? Tell me!"

As she spoke, her father's face went from angry red to sallow gray. He did not pull the flask back from Lily as he'd intended with his outstretched hand. His shoulders sagged and his head bowed forward.

"Tell me at once," Lily begged, not sure she really wanted to know.

"Who told you?" he finally asked.

"A boy from town. He's been coming around to help with the animals."

Her father shot her a quick glance, but he couldn't hold her gaze. He looked down again. "What did he tell you?"

"He said he didn't care that my mother had been saved from the noose. Then he ran away before I could ask him more." She took a long breath. "What did he mean?"

Will pressed the heels of his hands against his eyes,

and slowly sank onto a stool. "Your mother was to be hanged. I had no wife and no one would take me. Most would rather die than marry the executioner. But your mother, she took my offer to live a cursed life rather than to swing on the end of a rope. We were married and you were born."

"She cheated fate," Lily whispered, finally understanding her mother's words. "You saved her from her fate."

"That's what Allyce believed," Will said heavily. "I loved her." His voice broke. "As I love you. And yet there's nothing I can do to keep children from throwing rotten eggs at you or taunting you simply because you are my daughter. 'Tis truly a cursed life I have given you, God forgive me."

After a moment of brittle silence he asked, "Do you want to know why your mother was to be hanged?"

Lily shook her head. Stumbling backward, she made her way outside where she fled into the forest. At first she headed toward her mother's grave, but then she quickly changed her mind and veered away. She didn't care in which direction or whether she came upon a band of cutthroats. She just ran. She ran on until the pain in her side tore her breath from her and she could no longer fling one foot out in front of the other. She dropped to the forest floor, covering her eyes with her arm. Though she had run long and far, she hadn't outrun her thoughts. They came crashing against her.

Her mother was a condemned criminal!

Lily couldn't imagine her gentle mother standing on the platform with her hands tied behind her back whilst townsfolk threw curses and worse at her. Only her father's intervention at the last moment had saved her. A knight in armor black as death, her mother had called him.

Lily tried to imagine her father swinging his killing ax or pulling on the ropes, but all she saw was the vision from her nightmare of the tall and powerful stranger wearing a black hood.

Couldn't life be simple once again, when she believed that the condemned should die? When she imagined all criminals to be evil? When her father's duty to Lord Dunsworth was honorable and just? She knew her father only did his duty as executioner, but if someone as kind as her mother, no matter what her crime was, could be sentenced to death, how could he bear to live with himself? He was not the judge nor jury, but he did impart the final blow.

And she was destined to be his assistant. How would she ever be able to live with herself?

She spread her arms wide, fingers stretched as far as they would reach, wishing she had the wings of a dove with which to fly away.

CHAPTER NINE

Her father was not home when Lily returned. She paced from the hearth to the door to the apothecary, and back to the hearth again. Occasionally she stopped to add a log to the fire, or to peek out the front door, or to take a pinch of dried mint to chew on, but she couldn't concentrate on any one thing. She mostly dreaded her father's arrival, and yet she wished he'd come home soon. She had much to tell him.

Lily twisted her fingers together as she walked back and forth. Blossom yipped, calling for attention from her mistress. Lily knelt down and scratched her dog's belly as the pups jumped and nipped. Lily picked up her favorite pup. She loved the runt best of all because he needed her to feed him. He often followed her around while the others played together with growls and rough tumbling.

Now he licked Lily's nose and then tried to chew on it. All at once, she knew what she must do. She bundled up the extra nipples she had made, and dropped the runt into a small sack.

Outside, the afternoon sun glowed orange. She didn't have much time for her errand. Pulling the hood over her head she hurried into town. John had once told her he lived with his mother and father and two older brothers near the north wall, so she headed in that direction. She kept her head low, glancing up occasionally so that she wouldn't run into others.

The sack in her arms squirmed and whined till a cold little nose poked through the neck of her cloak and rubbed against her chin. She laughed quietly, not wanting to draw attention to herself. "Aye, I'll miss you, too," she whispered.

As she neared the north wall, she kept watch for John. His father was a tailor, and when she saw the sign hanging above a door, she knew she had found the boy's house. But now what? She had never visited another's home.

With a sigh of relief, she saw John walking down the road toward her, kicking a stone ahead of him.

As soon as he saw Lily, he stopped and glared. Then he ran away and slipped down an alley. Lily hurried after him.

"John, wait," she called.

The boy abruptly turned around. "What do you want?" He stared at her, anger and hurt pulling his face into a scowl.

Lily hesitated. How could she blame the boy? Last he'd seen her, she had been hurling rocks at him.

She brought the pup out from under her cloak. "This is for you." She held her breath and waited. What if he rebuffed her? What if he didn't want this gift?

John looked at her suspiciously. Then he looked at the pup and his expression softened. He took the runt from her hands.

"He needs extra care, and I don't have time to do it." She handed him the sack with the nipples. "You have to feed him twice a day, though he's nearly weaned."

"What's his name?"

"Whatever you choose," Lily said. She pulled her hood tighter around her face. "I have to go now. Take good care of him."

"Why are you giving him to me?"

"I've already told you," she said. "Because I am so busy in the apothecary. I have no time for him."

Lily turned and hurried to the end of the alley, looking both ways before stepping out onto the narrow road. John did not call after her. She walked quickly through the roads, only getting lost once as she tried to keep the setting sun to her right in order to find her way to the gates. As she left the town behind, she breathed easier and loosened her hood. She knew John would love and care for the pup. Still, sadness sat across her shoulders like a heavy yoke.

As she approached the cottage, she knew her father was inside. But now that he was home, she wasn't ready to see him. Stepping carefully, she crept to the side of the cottage. The dove cooed and the rabbits skittered in their cages. Since her mother had passed, Lily had taken in fewer injured animals. She simply didn't have the leisure to find and care for them.

Lily squatted next to the cages. Two rabbits, one dove, a quail, and the hedgehog were all that were left. First, she let the rabbits go. When she put them on the ground, they sat for a moment. Lily stomped right behind them and they hopped off and out of sight. Next, she carried the quail to a thicket at the edge of the forest. It would find its way in its own time, she knew. The hedgehog had lost a foot, but now he got around quite well. It shuffled off as soon as she released it.

Finally, the dove. Lily had removed the wrapping from its wing two weeks earlier. She had exercised the bird so it had stretched its wings to regain its power. The wing didn't look deformed, but that didn't mean the bird would be able to fly. So far all she had seen it do was flap from one perch to another as it strengthened its wing. Cautiously, so as not to alarm the dove, she reached in and caught it between her hands. She kept its wings pressed to its side so that it couldn't flap them in panic.

Lily carried the dove close to her chest and walked away from the cottage. She found a space where the trees were sparsely scattered. A perfect place to release the bird.

Holding her breath, she lightly tossed the dove up into the air. It spread its wings and flapped higher and higher, lifting Lily's heart with it. The bird was free. She, Lily Goodman, had healed it! The bird swooped out of sight. Gazing into the empty sky, she imagined herself healing not only birds and rabbits, but children with broken bones, and women who had trouble birthing babies, and even crabby old men who were careless with a whittling knife. She could do it. She looked at her hands in wonder, realizing they were no longer clumsy. Though not slender and delicate, they nevertheless held the power to heal.

Abruptly, she remembered her father. She could no longer put off going inside.

Lily hesitated in the doorway of the cottage before entering, still uncertain what exactly she wanted to say to him.

Will sat at the table drinking ale. He looked up at her uncertainly. "Where were you, child?"

"Just now I was outside freeing the animals. They're all healed. And the dove flew away." She couldn't help the pleasure that came out with her words.

"You have your mother's touch."

Lily heard the sad timbre in his voice as she hung her cloak on a peg near the door. She moved to push the pot of lamb stew over the fire and stirred it. Master Baker had given the meat in exchange for medicine for his wife.

"And I gave the runt to the town boy."

"Why? He was your favorite."

She paused in her stirring. The answer came as clear and pure as a bird's song, but the words would not come out. Lily let the question hang in the air until it was swept away by the sound of bubbling stew and the pups suckling in the corner. Her father didn't ask again, and though she tried for the rest of the night, Lily couldn't bring herself to utter the final words.

CHAPTER TEN

The next morning, Lily dressed carefully. She rubbed at the stains on her outer tunic, knowing the dress would never come clean in the King's lifetime, but feeling better for making the effort. She brushed her hair until it hung straight and smooth down her back, with no snarls marring its pale sheen. Her father met her at the door to the cottage. He wore a black cloak and the usual black gloves covered his hands.

"Lord Dunsworth has commuted the criminal's sentence," he said.

"He's not to hang then?" Lily asked hopefully, but her father's face did not lighten.

"He's to be executed by my sword instead. Lord Dunsworth took pity on the man's young wife who begged for mercy."

"Mercy?"

"Aye," he said gruffly. "For 'tis easier and more honorable to die by the ax than to be hung."

Lily took a deep breath to still the trembling that had filled her since early morning. A beheading. She tried to imagine the condemned man's wicked face, but all she could see was her mother's image.

"Come now," he said, picking up his sack of tools. "And follow close so you don't get trampled."

Lily hung back. "I cannot go," she said, her voice a scratchy whisper.

"You must, child!"

"But I do not wish to."

"Do you think I *wish* to?" Her father's voice rose. "Nay! 'Tis my duty as it was my father's before me! And now yours as well!" With that, he turned and strode on before her.

As always, duty compelled her to obey. Lily's legs carried her forward, though she longed to flee into the forest.

Her father led her through town to the platform erected in the middle of the square. Filled with deep dread, Lily followed him up the steps. He motioned for her to stop halfway and sit on one of the stairs.

Now that they had passed through the town, the crowd surged around like hungry wolves, howling for the sinner's blood. They pressed against the scaffolding holding up the platform, and Lily felt it tremble and shake. She worried it would collapse and drown her under piles of splintered wood. But perhaps that would be best.

Lord Dunsworth's men brought the prisoner out on a cart. As the cart wended through the crowd, boys threw rotten apples and eggs at the condemned man. He stood, tied to a post in the middle of the wagon, his head cast down as though in shame.

When he did look up, Lily steadied herself against the next step. This was no villain being trundled on the cart. He was a boy, just turned to manhood with fair whiskers only tickling his chin, and a bare chest and arms that had not yet developed the strength of a man.

Lily could hardly bear to look at him, yet she couldn't look away.

The jeers and shouts continued as the lord's soldiers roughly yanked the boy onto the platform and pushed him to his knees, facing the crowd, his hands still tied behind him.

A priest stood on the platform, his tonsured head

gleaming in the morning light. He bent low to bless the sinner one last time. Afterward, he rose and stepped aside, his hands clasped and his eyes closed with prayer. The executioner stepped forward.

Cheers erupted from the mob. "One cut! One cut!" they cried. Horrified, Lily realized they wanted the executioner to cut the boy's head off with a single swipe of his ax. The executioner, his head now covered in a black hood, revealed the shiny sharp edge of his ax.

With careful consideration, the executioner positioned himself behind the prisoner, lining up his blade next to the boy's bare neck. He moved easily, as though he were simply going to chop a block of wood. Then Lily caught the familiar tilt of his head and the shrug of his left shoulder. Lily stared in horror. Suddenly, he was not the executioner in black, the distant stranger pulling the ropes in her nightmares, *he was her father*.

She tried to tear her gaze away from the execution, but it snagged on the boy's face. Tears washed his eyes as he stared dumbly out at the people who clapped to see him executed. Lily tasted blood as she bit her lower lip. She wanted to clench her eyes shut to stop this from happening, but she couldn't even make herself blink. As though caught in a new and more terrifying nightmare, Lily watched.

Her father brought back his ax. The crowd fell silent. In one smooth arc, he swung the weapon forward, cleanly cutting through the boy's neck.

The impact of the blow knocked the head aside. But instead of landing neatly in the basket her father had placed for that purpose, it fell onto the wooden planking, rolled across the platform, and dropped to the uneven cobbles. Blood sprayed wide.

Someone pierced the air with a shrill scream. Suddenly everyone was running in panic, shouting and yelling with fear as mothers snatched up children and pulled them out of the way, and boys scrambled between legs to escape. The mass of people rippled like a single piece of cloth waving in the wind.

When the head settled in a ditch, the tangled crowd re-formed around it. Some were crying with fear because blood speckled their clothing.

Lily realized everyone was staring at her. She was the one screaming. She clamped her hands over her mouth.

As she watched, her father stepped off the platform with a pike in his gloved hands. Now he would carry the head to the castle gate, where it would be displayed to remind people not to sin against God nor King nor, in this case, Lord Dunsworth. And the head would remain until the birds picked it bare and the skull wobbled in a strong wind. Then it would fall and shatter on the stones below.

Lily lurched to her feet and stumbled down the steps. She did not dare look at her father.

Taunts and jeers echoed through the narrow roads after her as she ran away. "Lily White as Bones!" "Bloody Lily! Bloody Lily!" She ran and ran, the mocking cries growing distant as she neared the town wall.

No one stopped her as she rushed through the gate and down the dirt road toward home. Inside, she pulled at her dress. When it wouldn't come loose easily, she pulled harder, ripping the seams, but she didn't care. She flung the blood-spattered garment on the floor.

Naked, Lily grabbed a pitcher of water and poured it over herself. She scrubbed her hands and face, then she washed the rest of her. The rough cloth scratched her body and turned her skin a dull red.

Then she pulled her only other tunic on over her wet body. Taking the damp cloth, she wrapped the clothes into a bundle to feed to the fire.

Lily shuddered and crouched beside her pallet, hugging her folded legs close to her and burying her face against her knees. She sat dry-eyed, waiting.

Much later, she heard her father's booted feet approach the door. When it swung open, she rose and stared at him hard. For so many years the executioner had only been a dark figure in her nightmares, but now he was standing before her. And yet, she loved him.

He removed his gloves and placed them on their high shelf. He took a step toward her, holding out his hands. They were strong and wide. No blood stained the skin. She forced herself to take them.

As her father opened his mouth to say something, Lily blurted out, "I must go. I am leaving."

Will slowly closed his mouth. He withdrew his hands and filled a tankard of ale. "Where would you go?"

"I don't know. Somewhere . . . some place where no one knows who I am. Some place I can learn more about healing."

" 'Tis what your mother prayed for. What she dreamed of."

"But what of you?" Lily couldn't help asking. "What will you do? How will you manage? Perhaps I should stay." The words left her mouth before she could stop them.

"You must go."

"But who will assist you?"

Her father refilled his drink. "I will find an apprentice, the son of an executioner from another town."

"But who will—"

"Enough! You will go away from here. Gather your things and leave." He turned away from her and said over his shoulder, "You are no longer any use to me. I do not want you here."

The cruel words bit deep. Tears blurred her way as she hurried to secure a few belongings, including the mortar and pestle her father had given her, and her mother's finely carved comb. She tied it all into a bundle she could carry on a stick over her shoulder.

"Be gone," her father insisted when she stood uncertainly before him. He turned his face away. "Go."

❧   ❧   ❧

Lily fled, running away from her father and from her own betrayal. Even as she ran, she knew she should have stayed.

Without realizing where she was going, she soon found herself beside her mother's grave. Lily dropped her bundle and sprawled next to the stone.

She cried for a long time, hearing her father's words over and over again. *I do not want you here.* She would have preferred piercing arrows or stinging stones to those words.

Lily gasped. Words like stones. He had purposely struck her with evil words. He had chased her away because he loved her, just as she had done with the fox. She could return to her father and likely he would welcome her home, but that was not to be her fate. Her destiny lay beyond this forest and down a distant road she'd never seen, barely even dared imagine. Like the fisherman in her mother's dream, her father had set her free. And this time she was not running away but running toward her future.

EPILOGUE

Will stretched away from the trestle table, leaning his head back to relieve the tension in his neck. Each year it became more and more difficult to hunch over his herbs and concoctions.

He ambled outside, enjoying the fresh spring air. Without even thinking on it, he headed into the forest. In the two and a half years that Lily had been gone, he had found much solace beside his wife's grave. The path to her marker was well worn by now, but even in the dark he could have found it, the way was so familiar.

When he reached the graveside, he did not notice anything amiss at first. The gentle mound of earth had flattened over time, but he kept the area clear of dead leaves and undergrowth. He often brought flowers or willow branches to rest against the headstone. This time he had nothing to offer.

Not until he knelt beside the stone did he see the cross. It was the size of a child's finger, made of silver with intricate carvings along the edges. It hung from a delicate chain. Someone had draped the chain over the stone. Intertwined within the small loops of the chain were several feathers from a dove's breast.

Lily.

The grief overwhelmed him. Even right after she had left, he hadn't felt such a painful wrenching of his heart. The tears came without warning. Flooding his eyes. Filling his nose. Tears he had been saving his entire life, ever since he'd been a boy, teased and taunted and chased away. The executioner's son.

He gently touched the gleaming cross. The feathers fluttered with the movement. Lily was well. She had left the cross, he knew, to tell him so.

As his tears abated, he imagined his daughter in some distant part of the land, healing and soothing as Allyce used to do. Carefully, he lifted the cross from its resting place and hung the chain around his neck. He would keep Lily's gift next to his heart, where it would be safe.

AUTHOR'S NOTE

I've always been interested in medieval times. As a
child living in Belgium, my family toured many of
Europe's castles. The ancient, thick stone walls and tur-
rets, and the dank dungeons never failed to stimulate
my imagination. I became a princess or a knight in
shining armor. I battled dragons and always won.

My interest in medieval life never faded. As I grew
up, I continued to travel and visit castles. They still
held a magical appeal for me, but I also grew very aware
of the darker side of the Middle Ages such as the pesti-
lence, the harsh laws, the famine, the battles. The more
I learned about what life was like back then, the more I
wanted to know.

The Middle Ages ran from around A.D. 450 to A.D.
1500. During this more than one-thousand-year span,

England went through many cultural changes. In the earlier years, England was in transition from life under Roman rule to life under the influence of invading Angles and Saxons (from the coasts of Denmark and Germany). Then, in 1066, William, from Normandy, invaded and conquered England, thus giving him the name William the Conqueror.

Soon, England thrived, and the period known as the High Middle Ages began. New towns sprouted up; the merchant class could now afford luxuries such as elaborate wall hangings and glass windows instead of oiled cloth. The population was expanding, so more food had to be produced with the help of newly designed farming equipment. Soaring cathedrals and solid castles were built, many of which remain standing today. It was a time of growth and prosperity, except for the peasant class, which toiled from dawn till dusk.

Although many aspects of life were quite civilized, there was a hauntingly barbaric side—the punishment of criminals was far less humane than it is today. Thieves had their hands cut off; liars often had their tongues removed; criminals were tortured on the rack or the wheel. Yet everyone accepted this, for the most part, as a way of life.

Punishments were seen as a good deterrent against future crimes, and the criminals were portrayed as sinners who deserved to be humiliated, tortured, or executed. Children attended the executions with the rest of the townsfolk. There was much shouting against the condemned person and cheering for the executioner. And once the convict was killed, he was often left on display for people to see as a gruesome reminder not to sin.

Once the idea for this novel came to me, I started to do research into an executioner's life. On a summer vacation to Europe with my family, we visited the medieval town of Rothenburg ob der Tauber in Germany, and at the Kriminalmuseum I came across an intriguing book called *Criminal Justice Through the Ages*, which described the life of an executioner in a medieval town. Because his job was to kill for a living, people were both frightened and disgusted by him. As a result, the executioner was not allowed to attend church, drink in pubs, or fraternize in any way with others. And that was true for his family as well.

Many executioners inherited their job from their father, or were criminals themselves, given the job of executioner only to save their lives. Some were alcoholics, unable to bear what they were doing, but condemned to the profession nonetheless.

Because there were usually few executions each year, the executioner made extra money by working other jobs such as driving lepers from town and cleaning sewage cesspools. Or, as in Lily's father's case, by becoming a healer. There was a mystical aura surrounding the executioner. So much so, that people would visit him secretly for medicine, which they felt held more potency. Some believed that the rope used to hang criminals had special healing powers that only the executioner could pass on by way of his concoctions.

As I discovered more about the executioner's family "curse," I felt it was important to portray Lily as an outcast, as she truly would have been in 1450, the approximate date this story takes place. I imagined that life would have been extremely difficult for Lily, given her circumstances. But, like other women of her time who became leaders and surgeons and defended castles, I wanted Lily to choose to fight against her destiny—to rise above her fate.